I0574369

Written In The Stars?
Copyright 2025
Independently published by Briar Townsend
All rights reserved

No portion of this work may be reproduced in whole or in part without the express permission of the author. If referenced in another work, credit must be given. This work may not be used to train or inform artificial intelligence or related technologies. All rights remain with the estate of the author upon their death unless and until the copyright expires.

Written In The Stars? is a work of fiction. Any references, resemblances to, or mentions of real people, places, or things are either coincidental or fictionalised, and not intended as a realistic depiction or representation of said entity.

Cover art and design: Katarina Bajc

Print ISBN: 979-8-9923066-2-0

Written In The Stars?

a queer novella

by
Briar Townsend

Content Guidance

Written In The Stars? contains allusions to and mentions of transphobia and homophobia. Additionally, there are two distinct coming out storylines. While neither goes poorly, there is a fair amount of angst and self questioning.

One of the main characters lives with a well managed diagnosis of OCD. The other main character has anxiety that fluctuates from intense to negligible. These are not hidden or shameful identities for them, but the depictions may be close to home and I would not want any reader caught off guard.

This book also contains explicit sexual content. My style tends to be referred to as "comfort smut" and "homonormative." Be that as it may, if PG is your cup of tea, I am not the barista for you.

While generally a light hearted story, it's possible these topics may cause you distress. Please take the space you need before, during, and/or after reading to look after yourself.

TABLE OF CONTENTS

Before   1

Chapter One   17

Chapter Two   51

Chapter Three   95

After   129

BEFORE

Taking a moment to reflect during a slow day of work, James realises that his life is pretty close to perfect. Lost in his swirling thoughts, he hides away a private, sentimental smile by reaching for another glass and giving it a shine.

James is standing behind the bar of Paul's pub, tidying up before the mild rush that'll be coming in a few hours and assessing his young life as a way to occupy his mind. He chose this job because it gives him enough time to write, enough money to afford the flat he shares, enough flexibility to see his mates and go out, and not nearly as much stress as if he'd aimed for something more traditional in some sort of office. As a bonus, he genuinely enjoys the atmosphere, his coworkers, and getting to hear so many strangers' stories across the professional barrier of the bar.

It's not that he's planning working here forever, especially because it pays just barely enough for him to get by. But for now it's one piece of his nearly perfect life. He's only twenty five. He's got time.

James left uni a few years back and decided to stay in London both to pursue his writing and to live near his mates. London also fulfilled the requirement of existing close enough to his family back in Ireland that he never gets too overwhelmingly homesick, but far enough away from his brother and much of the extended family that he doesn't care for. It's a balancing act, but he thinks he's found the most stable option. He's happy here, living as he is, and with the people he cares about nearby.

Tonight's shift at the pub should be predictable and calm because it's the middle of the week. These nights are some of his favourite working hours. It's one of those pubs that has sports for those who fancy them, a few pub games for those who don't, and plenty of space for everyone to share. Paul's doesn't rely on any specific niche or theme, just the sort of comfortable, local place that people settle into.

Case in point: the slumped frame in the corner booth that belongs to one of his best mates, Karim. He'll come here occasionally as a sort of antithesis to the school he works at, marking papers while sipping a beer or two. Karim's a quiet, introverted sort of person, so James generally leaves him be whenever he stops by.

Though he wouldn't admit it readily, Karim prefers being near his friends (or quite literally in his husband's lap) even if he has work to get done. He likes to pretend he's all tough and whatever, but James knows the truth of him. Karim is a squishy, sentimental nerd who cares more than he ever lets on and comes round the pub more for James's presence than anything else.

Karim's husband, Arthur, is currently across the table from him engrossed in his own hobbies. Arthur's only here tonight to keep Karim company. The newlyweds started visiting the pub on weeknights when James mentioned how chill the environment tends to be and that Paul's is close enough to where they all live (only a few blocks apart from one another) that they can walk easily enough even when the weather's shit or they aren't up for dealing with the tube. It's nice to have somewhere to go after work that isn't just their flat, especially with a friendly face behind the bar.

Arthur's a paramedic and Karim teaches sixth form, so between the two of them, they're very dedicated and chronically overworked. Completely in love in a way that sees them through quite literally anything, they are always and forever each other's top priority..

James first knew Arthur as his uni flatmate. A few months later, he met Karim as the man who stole Arthur's heart with a smile across the classroom and never looked back. They don't come by James's work more than once a week or so, but he loves seeing them because with his own nighttime work shifts, Karim's long hours at school, and Arthur's chaotic schedule with the NHS, he'd only get to see them about once a month otherwise.

Besides the two bleary eyed nerds in the corner of Paul's pub, James is still close to Henri and Blair, and has been for roughly the same length of time. Their other uni friends have gradually drifted away, but the five of them haven't wavered. If anything, leaving school and choosing to stay mates in the "real world" solidified their group relationship in a more permanent way. When the time constraints of new adult life and the stress of it all start to catch up to them, they lean on each other instead of away, and now, about eight years into their friendship, they're all closer than ever.

James generally prefers his circle of trust to remain small. He makes friends easily, but he doesn't always keep them. He's got more acquaintances than he knows what to do with, and James could fill a room with his personal connections, but these few are the ones he really considers proper friends. Something closer to family at this point.

He's a bit…closed off, not in a way that's negative, but in the way that only certain people get to see the messy, unlikeable parts of him, and only after he knows they won't toss him out for it. And beyond his uni mates, there's only one other person he's chosen to include in his circle.

August is a bit younger at only twenty three. They've been living together since August left his own school days behind and James needed a flatmate to keep up with city living. He'd put out an advert, met with a few people who were decidedly *not right,* before finding August and feeling like they'd known each other in a past life (not that James believes in that sort of thing). They got on immediately, joking and chatting about sports and quite literally everything, up to and including their families, and August had moved into James's new flat only a few days later. It's been domestic bliss ever since.

James and August have completely opposite schedules, but they're both very tidy and well mannered and have a lot of the same interests. Even on a bad day, they still get on well and know when to give the other space.

August works at a cafe, but James knows that his real goal is to be a singer. And not even like a proper pop star or anything, he just wants to make enough money with his music to do it full time and maybe tour a bit. August is always singing around the flat, playing whatever gigs he can, and James goes to as many as he's able to offer his support, with their other friends tagging along for the occasional show.

And where August has his music, James has his writing. He went to uni for a literature degree, but the past few years he's been focusing on poetry. He jokes that it's because he's Irish and the lineage of Irish poets is too strong for him to aspire to anything else. His parents named him James Joyce Dolan for fuck's sake, predisposing him to a legacy he could never hope to fulfill. But the truth of his passion is closer to his obsession with word choice and metre and making words sing their way off the page to rest in the reader's soul.

James has written other mediums and genres, and he's published a few short stories that paid him almost literally nothing, but he's had no success getting his poetry picked up yet. He's determined that it will happen eventually if he stays focused. James knows he's got the talent and he works incredibly hard at improving his writing, so if he's patient, he thinks he's got a decent chance.

Recently he started a side gig writing drivel (or so he considers it) for an independent magazine, which he isn't exactly proud of but he's also not ashamed. Paid writing work is always hard to come by, so even if it's a small thing and not what he *wants* to be writing, he's glad to have it.

But August reads his real writing, the verses that come from his soul, the ugly drafts before they're honed. He encourages James when he fields professional rejections, and it's really nice to have someone at home after a bad day or a long night of work, even if they only see each other in the afternoons when their work schedules leave them both free most days.

August is the most recent piece of James's charmed life and he's the part that James is still figuring out. Blair and August hit it off almost as quickly as James had with each of them separately. James's other mates have their own friendship with August by now, always including him whenever James is invited because they like him just as well even if he's a newer addition.

It's just that sometimes James feels like he's missing something, and he only notices after certain conversations or interactions with August, never any of his other mates. It's an unnamed, hollow impression, some sort of lacuna that shows up once August has left James to go to a gig or visits his parents in Ontario for a few weeks a year and James occupies the flat alone.

The feeling doesn't bother James, exactly, but he notices that his days are immediately improved when August returns. Maybe they've grown codependent after spending so much time together. For now, it's not a huge concern since they're both homebodies who prefer their comforts and routines a majority of the time. But James does notice.

And speaking of August...

"Fancy seeing you here." The man himself drops into the seat nearest to where James has almost finished tidying away the glassware, Blair walking up just behind him and taking the next barstool over.

"Didn't expect you two tonight. Arthur invite you?" James tilts his chin in the direction of the Das-Anderson occupied booth where Karim is marking essays with an extremely dubious expression and Arthur is focusing hard on a sketch of Blair and Henri's kid: William (known as Junior to almost everyone). He's only a few months old, but he's the darling of the family, their mates, and literally everyone he meets. Arthur thought the picture would make a nice addition to Henri's desk at work.

"No, actually." Blair leans forward on their elbows and gives James a very tired smile. "Hen's home with Junior while I have a night off, so I asked August if he fancied a visit to those new gardens that just opened. I still have a bit of time, so August suggested we come by and visit you, grab a drink before we head home."

"And how were the gardens?" James asks, already reaching to pour each of them their usual: for Blair, a glass of red wine, and for August, tequila on the rocks.

"Gorgeous." August answers, waving over to Karim who's noticed their arrival and not so gently nudging Arthur to get his attention. Arthur startles, then gives a wave of his own, slowly emerging from his art project. Karim stares at Arthur with a far too fond expression given the circumstances before adjusting his glasses and getting back to work.

August turns back to James to continue his thought. "It'll be all tourists soon, so I'm glad we went when we did."

"I'm taking Henri and Junior next weekend. Bought a pass for the year." Blair accepts the glass from James with a grin and sits up from where they'd been slumped atop the bar. "You should come with us. August said he'd go again, and I'm sure Hen could convince those two. We should make a day of it, the seven of us."

"That'd be great, except not the next two weekends." James slides August his tequila, deciding at the last moment to sprinkle a bit of rock salt for added effect and to watch the way August's laugh works its way through him, starting with his eyes and eventually taking over his entire face. No one laughs at his nonsense quite like August. "Working eight days straight so I can get the next weekend off to see my mum for her birthday."

Blair looks between August and James while sipping their wine, an odd sort of expression on their face that they clear away immediately when they realise they've been caught by James.

What the hell is that about? For some reason they dart their eyes away and stand up to go visit with Karim and Arthur even though they just sat down, leaving James and August alone. The pub's still mostly empty and none of the other patrons need James at the moment. Even if they did, Paul's working with him tonight and he's more than happy to let James handle the washing up and focus on serving drinks instead.

"So how was it really?" James leans forward so that he and August are in a sort of private bubble, voices low while they talk. This is a thing they do frequently: waiting until the others are occupied and sharing the details they leave out from everyone else.

"I'm annoyingly allergic to every single flower, Blair spent half the time worrying about William, my feet are sore from accidentally walking in circles, but honestly it *was* gorgeous. Didn't lie about that part." August glances back at Blair where they've taken a seat next to Karim and started reading through the papers that have already been marked out of curiosity. "But mostly we just caught up. Talked for a while about...some things I've been figuring out. It was nice to get out of the flat and do something new. Get out of my own head a bit."

"I'm glad. I know things have been..." James isn't sure exactly what to say. August has been slightly off the past month or so and it's not that James is worried, but if August stays this way much longer he *will* start to worry.

Going out with Blair is only the second time he's left the flat for a reason other than work since he broke up with his last girlfriend. And it's not that the break-up was technically a catalyst for how August has been because he was already a bit off when they were together, but it was definitely a factor. "It's good to see you happy."

"Thanks, Jay." August sits back on his barstool and takes another sip of his drink, giving James a sideways sort of smile that doesn't quite reach his eyes. "You excited to be back in Bray for a few days? You haven't been since Christmas."

7

"I am, yeah." James starts wiping the bar even though it's barely been used since the last time he gave it a cleaning. It's an ingrained habit, especially when some nights it's so crowded he barely gets a chance. "I, erm, I won't be seeing Craig. Apparently after he and I fell out, he's now had a row with dad, and then had a go at mum, and little Bobby's barely older than Junior but he's already separating from his wife at her request and basically I'm hoping that my mum's birthday won't turn into a whole drama because Craig decides to show up and ruin the whole thing."

"Can't believe some of the things he's said to you." August shakes his head, scoffing. "You gave him more chances than I would've."

"Thing is, we used to be so close growing up." James tosses the rag into the pile for washing up and sets his hands on his hips while staring off at nothing in particular. "He was the person I admired more than anyone. More than my parents or my teachers or even my idols. But he's spent enough time ruining that. He's out of chances now, far as I'm concerned. It was one thing to have a go at me, but to blow up at the whole family like that…"

"Still the same bullshit reasons?" August asks, because while James has mentioned all of this before, he's usually hesitant to share specifics.

"He claims my parents getting divorced when we were young is the reason his marriage is failing. Something about setting a bad example, even though they still get on and they're both happier for it. Craig's just finding excuses to cause problems, I swear." James looks at August to roll his eyes. The audacity, honestly. Sometimes he wonders how he ever thought so highly of his brother. "But that's why mum didn't invite him to her party even though the rest of the family's coming in, including dad and Bobby with his mum. Fiftieth birthday's a big deal, but she said she'll not have Craig there unless he apologises to all of us, not just to her."

"I've met your parents, and if anything, they're the most amicable divorcees I've ever met. I'm glad you won't have to deal with Craig." August runs a hand through his chestnut curls to tuck an errant strand in place and James is glad to see he's got fresh marks on his hands that could only come from his guitar. That means he's playing again, which is a better sign than anything else so far. August had stopped practising for a few weeks, saying his heart just wasn't in it, so if he spent time today giving it a go, then that deserves to be celebrated.

"You've got a gig." James waits a moment to confirm his suspicion to avoid a jarring conversation change. It's a guess, but usually August tries to play a show every other week, more often if he's invited, and a new opportunity might have been enough to get the guitar back in his hands after the self-imposed hiatus.

"How'd you know?" August sets down his drink and gives James a surprised look, tilting his head to the left. That same curl he'd just tucked away falls loose again. He's like a stock photo from the 50s brought to life, sitting across from James with that natural charisma and effortless charm. The leather jacket only encourages the similarities.

"Guess I must be psychic." James laughs at the immediate eye roll from August as he reaches across to shove at James's shoulder with his own grin growing. It's so good to see him like this, even if he's still a bit dimmer than his usual bright self.

"It's Saturday and it's a small venue and I'm an opener for an opener but I'll get a portion of ticket sales which will probably end up being about 10 pounds but it's paid work and I need something easy to get my bearings so I've said yes." August sighs, something unnamed falling over him as he starts spinning his glass nervously. "Would you - I know you have work, but my set will be early in the night and you're working later so I was hoping you might be able to come?"

"I'll sort it out." James reaches out a hand to still August's anxious fidgeting. The gig will probably be before his shift, but even if there was overlap, he could make it work. "Wouldn't miss it."

"Yeah?" August looks up from where he's curled into himself. Quieter, he admits, "I'm really nervous. Played a practice set before Blair came by and I'm rusty."

"You'll be grand." James assures him, taking his hand back and glancing over at where the rest of his friends have now abandoned whatever work was being done to chat amongst themselves. If only Henri was here, they'd be all together.

Nowadays, with the Tompson-Storey baby and all six of them leading busy lives, they're rarely all in one place at the same time and it always requires coordinating their schedules.

James gives August his full attention, catching his amber eyes for a sideways smile. "And even if you're shit, I'll clap for you and whistle and make a fuss until everyone's convinced it's the best damn set they've ever heard."

"I don't deserve you." August sits up straight again, finishing off his tequila and setting the glass out of reach. "Add a water to my tab before I head home? Early start tomorrow."

"Go have a chat and I'll come round in a minute." James tilts his head in the direction of their friends, giving August an encouraging smile and the glass of water he'd already set aside. As if he's ever made August pay for anything when he visits, even if August was entirely joking about the water. James figures it balances out all the free shit August brings home from his own job.

James knows August well, knows his anxieties and his habits and the things that make him laugh. And August knows just as much about James because they spend time together basically every day. It's comforting to have someone like that in his life, especially as a flatmate.

He's grateful he found August, someone he can comfortably share his space with and hold a proper friendship. In his experience, it's usually one or the other, most people either orbiting around their flatmates but keeping significant personal boundaries or being best mates with them and not actually being very compatible at sharing the flat. But with August he's got both, and maybe two years after bringing him into his circle, he shouldn't still feel so much genuine love looking over at that booth where most of his favourite people are laughing together. But he does, because they're the best mates he could've ever hoped for and he's a lucky man to have them.

On instinct, James pulls out his phone, knowing that it's not actually unprofessional or anything since he's still technically doing the washing up and he's not needed elsewhere. Henri should be part of this even if he can't be here in person.

"Jay?" Henri answers just before the call would've gone to voicemail. If James had to guess, the phone is between his ear and shoulder while Henri holds Junior in his arms. "Everything alright?"

"Better than alright." James smiles, leaning forward on the counter to stare across at their friends. "Just having a bit of a moment and it felt wrong not to include you. Everyone else is here."

"Did you drag Blair in there? Arthur texted me a while back but I wasn't expecting them home for another hour or so." Henri shushes Junior for a moment, and his voice takes on this soft, soothing quality. He's such an incredible dad, and James is genuinely proud to know him.

"They showed up voluntarily. Brought August along, and now the four of them are huddled around a booth…I haven't seen August smile this much in months." James sighs, knowing he'll go over and join them for a few minutes before they all head home and leave him to the rest of his shift as it gets busy.

"It's good to see your boy smiling. Blair sent me a few pictures from the gardens." Henri offers as an explanation. James must be on speaker now because Henri's voice is slightly further away. "They tell you we're taking Junior soon? Blair wants us all to go if we can."

"Yeah, I think we should. Proper adults now, having babies and walking through posh gardens and that." James smiles wider as August and Arthur crack up laughing at something Karim said with a calculated smirk. Blair laughs softer, but they look tired which makes a lot of sense. Being a new parent is exhausting. "Can't for a few weeks because of my trip home for mum's birthday, but maybe when I get back."

"I've got to feed Junior in a minute, but send me a group picture, would you?" Henri's voice shifts again, this time to something nostalgic. Once William came home with them, they all knew nothing would be the same, but it was such a wonderful change that no one had it in them to feel resentful.

"Course I will." James stands up, starting to fix himself a soda water with lime to sip on while he joins their group at the booth. "Just wanted you to know I was thinking of you. Maybe Nana Pam or Auntie Jen want to look after the young sir for a night or two and we could all go out. In a few months, of course. Maybe when the weather's better."

"It's London. The weather's always going to be shit." Henri sounds like he's grinning at his own joke, and James misses him. He should definitely go over and visit their house soon. He can bring along the tiny football jersey he'd found for the baby and take William off their hands so they both can get a nap before they all catch up over a cuppa.

"You and Blair both home tomorrow?" James figures there's no need to wait. He's free in the morning and they live a bit further away than Karim and Arthur, but not by much. "Was thinking I could stop by after I wake up."

"We would all love that. Junior misses his Uncle James." Henri holds the phone up so that James can hear babbling, and it cracks his heart open in the best way. "If August isn't busy, bring him along."

"He'll be at work, but I'll pass along the invite in case he wants to drop by on his own." James knows he has to let Henri go, but he doesn't regret calling. If nothing else, it reminded him it's been a few weeks since he went over for a visit. "I'll see you tomorrow then."

"Text me on your way?" Henri asks, but before he hangs up, his voice goes all soft again to add, "Appreciate the call, mate."

"Love you, Hen." James runs a hand through his hair and grabs his drink, already moving away from the bar and signalling to Paul that he's taking a five. Paul nods his understanding and goes back to his conversation with one of their regulars.

"Love you too. Junior, say goodbye to your Uncle James." Henri lets Junior babble for another few moments before hanging up, James smiling at his phone before pocketing it and joining their friends.

He has to pull up a chair and move some things around (carefully, because there's student work and Arthur's drawings involved) to make room for his drink on the table, but he squeezes himself in and they include him immediately. Blair shows him a few of the pictures from earlier, Karim reads him a particularly *creative* passage from one of the essays he's marking, Arthur shows off his new sketchbook that he's been taking along on his quieter shifts to fill the time, and August waits until James joins them to tell everyone else about the upcoming gig.

James can only chat with them for a few minutes, but before he returns to work and everyone else starts assembling their things to leave, he shifts himself around to take a group selfie and sends it to Henri. He quickly gets a selfie of Henri with Junior in return, which he shows to the rest of them as he stands up to head back to work, grinning so wide his cheeks are starting to hurt.

"Wait - " August stands up and grabs James's forearm, following him a few steps away and back towards the bar. "I just wanted to, um, thank you. For the past few months. I know I haven't been myself and…"

James watches as August nervously runs his hand through his hair and holds himself hunched inward with his eyes downcast, like he's done something wrong. But he hasn't. He's entitled to spend time figuring out whatever it is he's figuring out, and it's not as if he's been difficult or anything. James has just been worried. "You don't owe me any sort of thank you, mate. I know it's been hard, even if I don't know why. I'm not your friend only when things are easy. Have my own dark days, as you know."

"I know." August glances up at him again and drops his hand from his hair. James follows it as it drifts back to his side, the faint marks of his guitar still present even from the bit of distance between them. James thinks August will be alright, but even if he's not, James will love him. They all will. "But I'm still grateful. I really am feeling better. I haven't exactly figured out everything that's bothering me, but I want to *try* again. I want music and time with friends and whatever else, which has to mean something. And I know it's at least in part because of all that optimistic faith you have in me."

"To be fair, you've more than earned it." James pulls him into a hug because he looks like he needs one. He won't pretend he isn't glad to know that August is feeling better, even if he's honest that he still has a ways to go. "You know you can always come to me, yeah? I may not be as therapeutic a presence as Blair, or oddly sage like Henri, and Karim and Arthur have been great as always, but I'm still here, too. Can't compete with Junior, of course, but then who can?"

August just nods against his shoulder while he listens and holds him a few seconds longer before stepping away from the hug and sighing. James gets a glimpse of their other friends over August's shoulder and finds them all staring. Blair looks conflicted, Karim is smirking, and Arthur flushes the moment James looks their way. He's not sure what that's about, but hopefully they haven't been gossiping about August's recent melancholy or anything like that. He'd be surprised if they were, but the thought still makes him bristle internally on instinct.

"I'll see you tomorrow, yeah?" James pushes his hands into the back pockets of his jeans and switches his focus back to August with a smile. "Told Henri I'd go over and visit around noon, but I should be home before you're off work. Maybe you could play your set for me?"

"That'd be great!" August brightens a fraction at the mention of getting to play for James. "I could really use the feedback. I think I need to adjust the order and maybe switch out one of the covers."

"We'll sort it out." James gives him one last shoulder squeeze before letting him go. August has an early morning and he doesn't want to keep him out late. "See you at home, Augie."

August nods and turns back to their other friends. Blair holds out his leather jacket with a questioning tilt of the head that August returns with a shrug as Arthur rushes to give James a hug goodbye before they leave.

James counts to ten after they're all finally outside with the pub door closed behind them, and right on time, Karim rushes back in, walks behind the bar like he belongs there, and pulls James into his own hug that's bracingly tight and immensely comforting.

"Come over soon, yeah?" Karim mumbles while still holding James close and swaying them on the spot. "Or we'll come over yours. Miss you…Love you."

"Love you too." James chuckles softly, patting Karim's back and holding him just as close. Karim's love is reserved, but the power of it could change the world. Sometimes, when he's nostalgic and thinking back on his life, James realises it already has. "Text me."

And then Karim rushes away like he's forgotten something, glancing back once he's at the door to give James one last, lingering look, then he's gone and probably outside with Arthur, snogging against the building just because he can. It wouldn't be the first time. Wouldn't even be the first time this week. James shakes his head at the thought because he really is so happy to have these people in his life.

"You good?" Paul gets James's attention from the other side of the bar. It'll be getting busy soon, or as busy as it gets on a Wednesday.

"Damn near perfect." James gives him a genuine grin and walks over to help Paul unload a crate they'd missed earlier. He works his shift and he chats with the customers and the whole time he's in his own head and his own heart, thinking about his mates, his family, his impending trip home, and his plans for the next few days. James wouldn't mind if his charmed life stayed exactly as it is.

CHAPTER ONE

A few months later…

It all started as a joke.

Technically it started as a job, but James didn't take it seriously. He's been known for his writing as long as he can remember, for his poetry, for his passion for the written word and for constructing language. He earned a degree and everything.

But his writing isn't paying his rent; his nights working at the pub take care of his living costs and he really enjoys his job. But the ad just seemed so inviting, so easy. Something he could do on the side while trying to get his first book published. And he could definitely use the extra money. He wasn't desperate, but he also needed to start thinking ahead about things like savings and unexpected expenses. So he reached out to the magazine with a few writing samples and within days he was set up with his new side gig.

The horoscopes practically wrote themselves.

Except they didn't, literally. James wrote them. He infused his natural humour and storytelling into them, thought of it like an exercise to keep his writing fresh while he saved his *real* writing for his many poetry collections and whatever other ideas caught his mind. James has fun with the horoscopes, never once spending the time to learn anything about astrology, but instead relying on his wit and rhythm to make it all sound very…worth reading.

It's been a few months since he started the magazine job, he's had no complaints, the checks keep coming in (meagre though they are), and he's started to look forward to the chance to explore his creativity. He hasn't mentioned it to any of his friends, except Henri, because no one can keep anything from Henri.

At first Hen was surprised because James has always been so against the idea of astrology, a disbeliever in fate or anything being predetermined or affected by heavenly bodies. But the long form "predictions" are posted in the online magazine, the daily horoscopes are cross posted on the various social media accounts, and it takes James only a few minutes a day, so once all that was explained, Henri understood. Financially, it makes sense.

But then Henri found out about a technique that James uses when writing the horoscopes. One very specific, tiny, insignificant aspect that James incorporated.

All the horoscopes he wrote were made up anyway, so what did it matter where he got the ideas?

Arthur never remembers to check the weather forecast, but Karim reads the horoscope over his morning coffee. After staying over a night at their place, James noticed that Karim shares the horoscopes aloud during their morning conversation. As a sort of test of concept, James posted a reminder: "*Virgo, don't forget your umbrella tomorrow. A storm is brewing,*" to save Arthur a soggy afternoon. He had confirmation later that day when they stopped in at the pub together, umbrella in hand.

And Blair always worries about parenting their first kid with Henri, assuming they're doing everything wrong even though the two of them are the most natural, loving parents James has ever known. So last Monday, James posted: "*Aquarius, you've done well today. Have a rest. You've earned it!*" He wanted to encourage Blair, even anonymously, and it had worked. Blair sent a screenshot to the group chat, saying it had been exactly what they needed to hear that day.

It's all generic enough that James can quietly reassure or remind his mates, knowing they'll see it on their social media, and without any of it being traced back to James. Blair even turned on notifications, telling Henri that whoever took over the account in March had a true gift. Henri, of course, choked on his tea while James glared at him until he reluctantly agreed with Blair. It's not that James is ashamed of his side job, but once he realised how much fun it could be as long as his friends remained clueless about the origins of their new favourite astrology account, he didn't want to ruin the mystique.

Henri let him get away with it for months. He would occasionally send James messages with screenshots of what he'd written for Capricorn, asking if it was supposed to be for him or for Karim (James would never answer and leave him guessing), and once even put him in a headlock for typing: "*Capricorn, it's only football. Remember to breathe and check your pockets.*" Because to Henri it was never just football and losing his third phone in as many years after a particularly exciting match was completely understandable. Besides, he heard about it often enough from his spouse.

And it wasn't only James's uni mates who inspired his horoscopes. August has been his flatmate for a few years, so it's only natural that James would post for him like he does for the others. James got away with that too, for months, until Henri discovered August's star sign and invited himself over to James's flat while August was away at work to confront James about the contents of his... *advice.*

"Mate, I mean this in the most sincere way possible: what the fuck is this?" Henri turns his phone around across the kitchen table, showing James an entire gallery of screenshots from the magazine horoscope twitter account.

James wonders where Henri found the time, between taking care of the baby and his job at the local charity where he's been required to work odd hours even before he and Blair adopted their first kid.

"My work, I assume." James glances briefly at the phone before focusing back on his laptop.

He's busy deciding on the order of a few poems in his next collection. After several unsuccessful attempts at finding an agent over the last year, he'd retracted his submission and taken it apart, determined to improve the contents and give himself a better chance in the second round. James already added a few poems, rearranged the order

19

multiple times, and made significant changes to the originally submitted work, keeping the unaltered file as a reference. But it's not ready yet.

"James. Focus. Look at my beautiful face." Henri waves, trying to get James's attention away from his laptop. He's hard to distract when in writing mode.

"What? I only vaguely hinted to Karim that he's about to forget his anniversary. Nothing too bold." James rubs at his eyes beneath his glasses. He was up late last night, later than usual. There'd been a birthday group at the pub who'd paid extra in advance to stay past closing, and he was one of the lucky few who was scheduled to stay and serve them. At least he was paid well for the extra work.

"No, not that. I took care of it. Arthur's got a new necklace coming his way and Karim thinks it was his idea. Maybe if they didn't celebrate three different anniversaries he'd have an easier time remembering, but I'm not any better." Henri leans forward and closes James's laptop over his fingers, retreating at the look of absolute scorn shot his way.

"You're lucky that's on autosave." James leans back in his seat and crosses his arms over his chest. He never minds a visit from Henri, and it's been a few days since they last saw each other, but he only needed a few more minutes alone with his writing. Alas. "What'd I do this time?"

"Augie's birthday is August 18th." Henri starts, his voice trailing as if his conclusion is obvious. But James doesn't have a clue what he's on about and just waves a hand indicating he should continue. "Which is a bit on the nose for his parents to be naming him August, but it also makes him a Leo."

"Why do I feel like I'll need a drink after this?" James stays closed off, not liking the way that Henri's tone has shifted to something warm and soft, like he's worried of scaring James off. Last time James heard that tone, it was after he had that falling out with his older brother, when Henri was the first one he called for support.

"Well…Blair is the one who brought it up. They haven't figured out your secret identity, don't worry!" Henri reaches out a placating hand when James looks vaguely panicked. "They were looking at some friendship compatibility thing and mentioned offhand how August was a fire sign and all that, and apparently a 'stereotypical Leo', whatever that means."

Henri's air quotes always manage to be exceptionally camp.

"Haven't a clue." James shrugs, no closer to figuring out why Henri is here, in the middle of a Tuesday, giving him some sort of *talk*. "My lack of astrological understanding doesn't impede my paycheck, so."

"Right, okay, but once I knew…I got curious. Figured you may have done with August what you've done with the rest of us. Cuz like August is such a horoscope girlie, yeah?" Henri waits for James to nod his agreement. August is very much a horoscope girlie and has been as long as James has known him. "Does August read your posts?"

"He does…" James confirms, still unclear where this conversation is headed. "He's the reason I found out about the job. Mentioned it to me one day when he got home from the cafe."

"And does he know you took the job?" Henri leans back in his seat, posture much more relaxed than James. But in James's defence, he's starting to feel like a cornered man. It's like he can see the trap being laid out but right now it's just a blueprint. When Henri really focuses on something, there's always a reason.

"Course not. Our schedules are different enough. He's never home when I'm writing for it, and it hasn't really come up when we hang out." James takes his glasses off and rubs at his eyes again. Maybe he'll treat himself to a nap before tonight's shift. "Is there some sort of point? This isn't even edging, Hen, just annoying."

"Calm your tits, I'm getting there, just trying to be a decent lad about it." Henri scratches at the hair on his neck, staring vaguely into the living room like he's searching for his words. James may be annoyed at the moment, but Henri is like a brother to him. He'll patiently wait for whatever this is, knowing Henri as well as he does and willing to trust him with his life. Or his afternoon, in this case.

"I'm making tea. You want?" James stands up from the table and walks past Henri, squeezing his shoulder in passing. "Know you've mostly switched to coffee in the mornings because of Junior, but you still go for an afternoon cuppa, yeah?"

"Cheers." Henri also gets up from the table, moving himself to the sofa rather than the kitchen. It's a small flat, just large enough for James and August to each have their own tiny bedroom and a minimal amount of common space, but it's cosy and organised and it works for them. They're not exactly flush, James's job at the pub and August's at the cafe nothing to write home about. But as they both have aspirations to other pursuits, it works for now.

"Right. Talk." James walks into the living room and sets the tea tray down on the coffee table, dropping himself on the sofa beside Henri and throwing an arm across the back. "Spit it out."

"Prefer to swallow." Henri cackles as James rolls his eyes, shoving at Henri with his foot until they're both laughing. He can always count on Henri to go for the gay joke.

"Good for you. I'll bring a pineapple next time I visit." James waits, once again motioning for Henri to get on with whatever it is. He's not usually so reluctant to have serious conversations, which apparently includes this.

"So, uh, your posts. About August." Henri takes his phone back out of his pocket and hands it over so James can read what he's talking about. "Do you…notice anything?"

James takes the phone and gives the screenshots a perusal. Nothing out of the ordinary, really, just vague advice. Sure, some of it was more pointed, more aimed at August specifically, without naming him of course. But that doesn't explain why Henri thought it was necessary to screenshot the posts and interrupt his writing time. "Nothing stands out, no."

"Maybe…imagine reading them to August. Or like think of the headspace in which you wrote them." Henri prepares his own tea while James frowns but does as Henri requested.

"Pour for me?" James settles into the corner of the sofa to truly focus. He finds the first screenshot, what looks like the oldest, and starts from there, wondering if he'll be able to convince Henri to just fucking tell him already instead of whatever this method is.

Has he been rude? Too overt with his advice? When Henri's brought up his horoscopes before it's been a passing comment while they chat over coffee or watch a footie match. It's not usually such an ordeal.

Leo, you're too good for them by half. You deserve someone who awakens that sunshine smile and inspires your dreams.

Leo, your laugh is like the stars. You're an entire constellation when you're happy. The night sky envies your light.

Leo, look around you. When's the last time you went outside? Fresh air will do you good.

Leo, you won't find what you're looking for sitting at home. Accept your friends' invitations to connect. They miss you.

Leo, you can be so stubborn when you're passionate. Give yourself a few days off from work. You've earned a break.

Leo, your voice will move mountains someday. Keep going.

Leo, let your friends help you sometimes. You don't have to do it on your own.

Leo, there's a reservoir held behind your eyes. Lean on Virgo. They've got your back.

Leo, your soul is like the sun. You have a gravity that can't be taught. Some day, everyone will see.

Leo, never forget who you are. King of the jungle, leader of the pride.

And on and on, until James scrolls through about two dozen. It's a daily posting schedule, and it seems Henri's picked a selection starting from the time he took over the account. James knows exactly what inspired each of the posts, but he doesn't see how any of it's related. While reading, he mentally scrolls through the past several months of life at the flat, which doesn't lead him to any sort of conclusion.

"Not sure what I'm looking for, if I'm honest." James hands Henri's phone back and accepts the mug offered in return. They've been friends for so long that it's more like being with family. Actually, he'd rather be with Henri than most of his relatives so in many ways he's more comfortable.

"You don't notice anything?" Henri gives James a very appraising look of disbelief. James feels intentionally observed and *seen* and it's making him squirm.

"I don't, no." James takes a drag from his mug and sighs, setting it atop his thigh and cradling the space by the handle with his overworked fingers. He really should stretch out his hands between intense writing sprints.

Henri nods at James's answer, stands up, paces back and forth twice, then sits down facing James with his lips pressed together. "Are all of those posts for August?"

"Think so, yeah. He's the only Leo I know, or at least the only one actively in my life. We live together, so it's pretty easy to see what sort of day he's having and post something to cheer him up or whatever the mood calls for." James crosses his legs, one knee atop the other, and waits for Henri to get to the point. This is taking longer than he thought.

"Which - er - what inspired the posts?" Henri scrolls through the screenshots for a moment until he's at the beginning, showing James the post about how August could do better than that woman he was seeing. "This first one?"

"That was when he was near the end of things with Martha. She never treated him right, always cancelling on him at the last minute, that sort of thing." James bristles at the memory of the morning that brought him to write that specific horoscope. "The day I wrote that one, Martha had spent the night after one of his open mic performances, and the next morning she was making fun of his set, saying he sounded off key and looked awkward on stage. Which - it's just - he fucking smashed it, obviously. You know what his voice is like."

"I do." Henri nods, still staring through James's soul with enough intensity to peel him apart, one layer at a time.

"Right. Voice of an angel and a natural performer at that. But even if it'd been a shit set, he wouldn't deserve that. She was walking around our flat, being all condescending and telling him he needed to grow up and give up on his singing and get a real career and all that shit." James runs a hand through the front of his hair and taps his fingers against the mug in agitation. "Hen, he's only twenty three and he has more talent than half the industry. I couldn't handle it without telling her off so I went in my room and let them have it out in private. Well, as private as you can get in this flat."

"They split up that day?" Henri generally keeps up with August's life, but none of them can be expected to know him as well as James. They live together and they're close friends. Blair has bonded with

August almost as much as James during the two years they've known him, but they're not here at the moment to fill Henri in on the specifics.

"Few days later, yeah." James gestures at Henri's phone. "Which is where that next one came from. We had a proper lads night for the first time in ages. Went out to a new pub across town, caught a match while we were there, came home and chatted for hours before we called it a night. It was the first time I heard him laugh in weeks. He'd been miserable, and he sort of fell back into his depression again on and off for a while. You probably remember. He's good now, though. Just needed a bit to find his footing again and work through some things."

"Right." Henri nods, sinuous fingers worrying at his own chin, clearly deep in thought. And then, "Jay, you know how you're straight?"

James laughs, surprised by the question, setting his tea down on a coaster and swatting Henri on the chest as he sits back up. "Oddly enough, I do remember being attracted to women. That's sort of the point of the shagging and the dating and all that."

"And you know how all your mates are queer?" Henri stands up again, hands in his pockets like he's trying to hold himself back from something. "Like…all of us. Me and Blair and Arthur and Karim, even a few of your lads from back home. Could hold your own Pride parade…you ever think about that?"

"About what?" James laughs again, pulling on Henri's elbow until he falls back onto the sofa. "I don't care that my mates are shameless cock sluts. You all remind me often enough that it'd be hard to forget."

"You have no thoughts related to that information?" Henri asks yet again. James is starting to suspect where this is headed.

They haven't had this conversation since they were teenagers let loose in London for the first time, back when Henri hadn't found Blair

26

yet and their demographic of interest was split. So James went along to gay clubs and Henri braved a few straight ones, each of them finding someone to take home every few weeks. James showed up to uni without knowing a single person and left with four of the best mates he couldn't imagine his life without, and those friendships had been forged over questionable decisions and copious amounts of vodka even if they've developed well past that stage.

"No?" James has never questioned his friends' identities.

Arthur thought he was straight when they first met, but that changed when Karim tagged along to the pub with Henri a few months into their first year after a chance encounter after class. And then James became the token straight friend, but it's never been an issue. He goes along to gay clubs and celebrates Pride with them and shows up to drag brunch and all the rest. They're his mates, his favourite people in the world. Why would it matter that they're queer?

"August is straight though, so not all my mates." James adds after far too many silent seconds.

"Right, August, yes, back to him." Henri leans forward and takes James by the shoulders, his hands holding James very firmly in place. "You love his laugh and you smile talking about his voice and you celebrated when his last relationship ended and you wait for him to come home from work after every shift. You encourage his singing and post on your horoscope account to make his days better. Do you see where I'm headed with this?"

"He's my flatmate and one of our friends. We wouldn't be living together if I hated the guy." James takes Henri's hands and drops them back in Henri's own space. If only getting him to drop the topic was so easy.

"When does August get home today?" Henri continues facing James but keeps his hands to himself. If James wants space, he'll respect that. Unlike the rest of their codependent circle, James is only in the mood for cuddles occasionally.

James checks the time on his phone, mentally calculating August's commute. "About twenty minutes. Shift just ended. Which is why I was getting some writing done before you showed up."

"Tell me about when he gets home from work and you spend time together. You're a writer, yeah? Describe it to me." Henri licks his bottom lip before biting it between his teeth, eyes not leaving James's face. He seems to be trying to prove some sort of point.

"He walks in singing if it's been a good day, silent and withdrawn if it's been stressful. Leaves the leftover pastries on the table and heads to the kitchen to get plates for the both of us in either mood. Then we usually chat while we have our afternoon snack. He tells me about his morning shift and I tell him about work the night before. Sometimes we make plans for the weekend." James shifts uncomfortably, knowing how it sounds even though it's entirely platonic.

He doesn't *wait* for August like some abandoned puppy. James just likes his company and it's nice to have someone to talk to. And the leftovers from August's work are practical as well as delicious. They save loads on grocery orders, never having to buy bread and enjoying plenty of snacks on hand if they get peckish.

Henri listens, nodding along and giving James another very calculated look. He considers for a minute in silence while James fidgets with the nearest cushion. He doesn't like feeling so observed.

"Jay, what do I smell like?" Henri's question surprises James out of his thoughts, bringing a laugh to the surface as he gives Henri a confused smile.

"How the fuck would I know? Probably like baby vomit and cigarettes these days, but I'm not walking around sniffing you. What a weird question." James laughs again, taking up his mug and swirling the contents before having another sip. It's cooled off, but still good. Still comforting.

28

"And August? What does he smell like?" Henri interrupts James before he can balk - "Just answer the question, mate. You live with the guy, yeah? What does he smell like?"

Glaring, because he definitely knows what Henri's getting at, James realises he does actually have an answer ready. "After work he smells like espresso and butter, like he brought the cafe home with him. And before a gig, he showers as like a nervous thing, so he'll be all fresh cotton and that cologne he always wears. Keeps it on his window sill because it's got some special rock inside the bottle and he says it has to charge in the moonlight? I don't fucking know. But most of the time he just smells like...a lad? Just like himself, I suppose."

"And what does Arthur smell like?" Henri finally picks up his own mug again, but he doesn't drink from it. He just toys with the handle and waits for James to keep talking. "You've lived with him, that first year at uni."

"I don't know, it was ages ago. The place was a tip. Suppose he smelled all sweaty after his runs but once Karim was involved he started caring a bit more so I guess he showered right after exercising and used some like minty body wash. Think Karim brought that though. Hardly a shower they didn't take together." James shrugs, unbothered by the memories.

He loved living with Arthur, but it became clear after a few months of Karim in Arthur's life that their living situation had to change. They wanted their space as a couple and James wanted space to be a messy single lad bringing people back from the club without worrying about interrupting them.

"So, just to summarise, August smells good and you like his voice and compliment his smile and wait for him to come home from work and use your astrology posts to make him feel better and celebrate his breakups." Henri waits for James to nod.

He's reluctant to agree, but Henri hasn't said anything untrue. Hearing it the second time is worse than the first, because he knows how it sounds and he can't deny any of it.

"I'm straight, Hen, as you've so recently reminded me." James knows that Henri means well, but just because all his friends are queer and he has an attachment to his flatmate doesn't change that fact. "I've not fallen for August."

"And you'd be totally fine with him taking up with some new bird and bringing her around the flat?" Henri has one eyebrow quirked, like he already doesn't believe the answer James is about to provide.

"August can date whoever he fancies. He's just been busy recently, with extra hours at the cafe and trying to get his music career going. As long as he finds someone who treats him well and supports his passion, I'll be glad for him." James won't admit it to Henri, but he does feel something like apprehension when thinking about the possibility of August in a new relationship.

It's just…he's met the sorts of women that August dates and most of them don't have a clue what an amazing partner they have. It's hard for James to watch as someone with August's sincerest best interest at heart. He deserves better.

"And the fact that you already fit that criteria means nothing?" Henri smirks, seemingly moving past his hesitation from earlier and just blatantly insinuating that James has feelings that he's denying. He took a fucking difficult path to get there, but James has finally figured out the point of this visit.

"I'm not dating August. We're both straight. Doesn't matter if I'd be a good boyfriend, because that's a given." James grins, gesturing at himself while Henri rolls his eyes. "There's nothing going on there. We're just…keeping each other company. We're young and busy and we're struggling artists with a lot in common. Course I want to spend time with him."

"You want me to drop it?" Henri is back to serious mode, hanging on James's answer like he's hoping for a response that James can't give.

"There's nothing to drop. But since you're here, catch me up on Junior and let me worry about who I'm pulling." James picks up Henri's mug and hands it back, putting a cap on the conversation and transitioning them firmly to a new topic. Henri is always happy to talk about his kid.

***

Exactly on time, the sound of August's singing enters the room as his key unlocks the flat's front door. James smiles about August having a good day at work before he catches himself. He doesn't miss the smirk Henri flashes his way or the heat flooding his own face at the insinuation. So he's observant. It doesn't mean he has a thing for August.

"Oh, hey Hen!" August catches sight of the two of them on the sofa and brightens even further. He loves having company. "You staying for a while?"

Henri gives James a very meaningful look, earning himself a shove and a scoff. "Nah, mate. Have to head out. Was just stopping by on my day off. Blair is at a mummy and me dance class with Junior and I'd like to be there when they get home."

"Tell them I say hello?" August drops today's box of pastries on the kitchen table as James gets up from his spot at the sofa, taking the tray with their empty mugs and the rest of the accoutrement to clear it away.

"Course I will. You and James want to come over soon?" Henri smacks James on the bum in passing, making him yelp and curse, almost dropping the tray. "Junior misses you."

"*Goodbye*, Henri." James sets the tray down and pulls Henri into a hug that's marginally too tight to be comfortable. Henri is never subtle and James doesn't want August to pick up on any weird vibes. "We'll text Blair to set something up."

August takes his usual seat at the kitchen table once Henri's out the door, setting a plate for each of them and waiting for James to join him. It's their routine.

"Good day at work?" James asks, already knowing the answer. August's rendition of *Dancing In The Dark* as he traipsed inside gave James more of a window into August's morning than he'd ever admit to Henri.

"The best!" August slides the box of goodies across the table towards James, giving him first pick. He always does. "But tell me about Henri. How's he been? How's William?"

"Junior's perfect, of course. He showed me pictures from the park yesterday. Kid's still got those cute little rolls on his arms and legs but he'll be crawling soon and he'll lose them. For now, he looks like Colin the Caterpillar, or that one from *Bug's Life*." James grins despite himself. William is more loved than he'll know what to do with as he grows up. "But I'll let Blair fill you in when we figure out dinner or something. Tell me about work. You get another gig?"

The thing about sitting here with August is that James does see what Henri is getting at. Now that the idea's in his head, he can't really turn off the thought that this isn't entirely a platonic way to live with a flatmate, at least not for most people.

He knows that August is stunningly pretty for a lad, but James doesn't have to be gay to see that, just human. And he does love their daily routine of catching up while sharing their afternoon meal, the liminal space between August getting off work and James leaving for the pub spent together almost every day. But it doesn't have to mean anything beyond companionship.

Except James catches himself staring more than once, and August keeps giving him this *smile* that feels private, just for him, and there's a pride that swells his chest every time he gets August to laugh, and something about the whole of it feels important now that he's let himself notice. These moments of shared life are more than nothing and he almost resents the fact he downplayed it for Henri. These afternoons together are important, a special part of his day that he wouldn't want to go without.

But they're just close friends.

And the horoscopes are just…how he writes. He's a romantic. He romanticises everything: breakups and meet cutes and sad commercials on the telly. Just because August has needed some cheering up the last few months doesn't mean he has feelings for him. Not romantic feelings. James just wants August to be happy. What sort of person would he be if he didn't want one of his best mates to be happy?

"Jay?" August tilts his head and looks at James under his eyelashes. Clearly he missed something in the conversation.

Maybe he shouldn't even be noticing August's eyelashes. Maybe he shouldn't be staring into August's eyes just because they caught the sun. Maybe Henri had a point.

"What? Sorry, lost in my thoughts. You were saying?" James runs his fingers through his hair, stopping when he realises he has flakes of pastry clinging to his hand. Why does he feel so jittery? "Ah, no. Ruined my famous quiff."

August stands up enough to reach across and pull a large chunk of croissant from the side of James's hair, tossing it away with a laugh as he sits back down. James wouldn't usually think anything of the physical contact, wouldn't usually question how easy and natural it was. He still doesn't think it meant anything, not properly. August's straight. He's straight. He's just caught up in what Henri said, that's all this is.

But if he's honest with himself, reluctantly, hesitantly honest, his own flushed cheeks and inability to focus when August does something like that aren't new.

It's in the way he knows August's hands. The familiarity with August's voice, both when speaking and his remarkable singing range. His fondness for August's smile that he always looks for across the table. How James's first thought, always, is August, whether to share a story from work or a frustration with the world. The way he looks forward to August getting home every day, always tidying up and making sure he's available unless he absolutely needs to make an appointment for himself. How when his friends invite him to anything, August is included by default, as in *you and August should come* or *are you and August busy that night* like they're a set. The way he's never corrected anyone because they weren't wrong in their assumption.

That hollow, emptied out feeling whenever August is away that disappears the moment he's back. James never quite figured it out, no matter how many times he hugged August goodbye and waited for him to come home.

Fuck.

***

What James often resents about himself is that he's very prone to thought spirals. It's the way his brain works, but he still wishes it weren't so easy to fall into. He has obsessive compulsive disorder, but not in any way like the stereotypes in the media would make it seem. He's tidy, but his compulsions are more mental than anything. Once he's in a thought spiral, it's very very difficult to get himself out, even with therapy and strategies in place to help.

So the fact that James has been obsessing over the nature of his relationship with August for the last fortnight is about 80% Henri's fault, 15% James's OCD, and 5% August. Because August is all the things that Henri pointed out and significantly more.

August *always* smells nice, and now that James pays attention, he finds comfort in it. His smell is familiar and homey, something James immediately associates with their shared flat. James hadn't realised before how he lingers when they hug, how he searches for traces of the bakery clinging to August's clothes or waits for hints of August's cosmetic use to know how worried he is before a gig (and then adjusts his support accordingly).

August's smile is a miracle. He could power a country with its charm. And his laugh is a music all its own. James watched an old video of their friend group, something from Blair and Henri's baby shower months ago, and he could hear August off camera laughing at whatever Karim said. His stomach did something horribly pleasant and warm at the sound so he tossed his phone onto his bed before shutting the door and busying himself in the kitchen, far away from that feeling. Unfortunately, the distance wasn't a cure.

The horoscopes continue. They have to. It's James's job and while the money isn't great, he can always use it. His paycheck from the pub is steady, but for all the extras and the unpredictables, he needs the little he gets from the magazine. And now that he knows Henri is looking for something in his not so subtle messages to August, he thinks twice about the contents.

James is still using all of his friends as inspiration. Not in a rude or exploitative way, of course. Sometimes it's just reminders that they're lovely and attempts to make their day brighter. But with August, even James can now acknowledge it's on a different level.

His spiralling is making him self conscious and jittery and flushed around his flatmate, but August hasn't said anything and nothing's happened between them so it's fine.

Everything's fine.

Until a Saturday night a few weeks after Henri's impromptu visit. James is at work, of course, and August is performing an important gig at some tiny venue across town. It was a last minute thing because of a cancellation. And James wanted to be there, but August understood that he had to work, saying that James couldn't take off every time he performs and that he'll tell him all about it tomorrow.

James checks his phone more often than usual that night, knowing that August is nervous because he'd stopped in at the pub for a pre-show drink to calm down, and for a pep talk from James. He comes to James when he needs to be steadied, and James pointedly doesn't make tonight's visit about him and his...feelings?

Whatever's going on with him, August has a big night ahead and that's what's important, not the way James's chest soars when August walks through the door, or the ease he felt when they hugged before going back to their respective sides of the bar to finish talking.

Where James has his OCD, August has anxiety. Crippling sometimes, even with treatment, but he's doing really well and James reminds him of that while he sits across from him and sips at his beer. August smells of shower gel and curl enhancer and James flushes when he notices himself settling into the fragrance like Winnie the Pooh floating after a honey pot.

But August's visit to the pub was hours ago and James has mostly gotten lost in work and moved on. Saturday nights are always the busiest.

It's well after midnight when James gets *the text*. His conversation with Henri is immediately on his mind as he reads August's message. James feels like he's failed some sort of test as disappointment and irritating heat flood his body.

No no no no no no no - the spiral starts too easily, a panic about too many things to name tightening his chest as his mind whirls beyond his control.

36

August: *Just letting you know I'm bringing someone back with me. I know you're at work for a few more hours, just didn't want it to be a surprise since she's probably staying the night.*

August: *My set was incredible! One of my best yet. Can't wait to tell you all about it :) Thanks for the pep talk and for everything else. Couldn't have done it without you!*

James stares at both messages for a length of time he's slightly ashamed of until Paul gets his attention to serve a group waiting for him at the end of the bar. He pockets his phone and goes back to work, unable to respond even if he wasn't busy.

James hates this feeling of being unable to control his own thoughts and he hates knowing there's fuck all he can do about it. Being mentally ill is manageable until it's not, but he's not to that point over this. Not yet. And he doesn't plan to let it get that bad if he can help it.

Henri was right. He was fucking right and James can't have an identity crisis in the middle of a pub, surrounded by strangers and coworkers who don't even know him.

James has feelings for August. James, a straight man, has feelings for another straight man. His flatmate, no less.

He's fucked. He's beyond fucked. This was never meant to happen.

He's not even gay.

But he knows deep in that spot in his gut that his spirals always narrow towards that his sexuality definitely isn't straight, and what the hell is he meant to do about that with his phone burning a hole in his jeans and Paul giving him concerned looks every few minutes when he zones out and knocks into the counter?

Drifting weightlessly through the last few hours at the pub, James serves drinks and smiles at the customers as if nothing is wrong, but internally he's a mess. His breathing is shallow and his mind is nowhere near work and he's doing his best to just get through the rest of his shift and then he can actually deal with this.

He's always known he was straight. With all the gay clubs and Pride events he attends with his mates he's even tried a few things with men. Snogging, a bit of over the clothes touching, but none of it ever did anything for him. Was he fairly wasted all those times? Sure. But he's twenty five. If he was going to have a sexuality crisis isn't he like a decade late to it?

"Pick up pick up pick up pick up pick up - Arthur!" James holds his phone to his ear as he leaves work, waving goodbye to Paul and Nicki who head the opposite direction to the tube. He should be on his way to his flat right now, but he can't. Just thinking about it made him dry heave over the sink, his body reacting to all of the *too much* that he can't process properly.

"Everything alright?" Arthur's voice has a filter of mild panic, and James can't blame him. He hasn't called Arthur in the middle of the night since…ever. But Arthur works late sometimes and James is literally praying to a god he doesn't believe in that tonight is one of those nights.

"You working? Off soon?" James leans against the wall outside the pub, free hand fiddling with a bit of lint in his pocket. He doesn't know where he'll go if Arthur's working through the night because going home is *not* an option. Maybe he could stay at Arthur and Karim's flat anyway? He can't wake up Blair and Henri. They barely get any sleep nowadays as it is.

"Just finishing up a few reports. Standard Saturday, nothing wild." Arthur still sounds hesitant and definitely tired. He's relatively new to being a paramedic, stuck working night shifts a few times a month, but he doesn't complain. Arthur sincerely loves his job, saving lives, being there for people in their most vulnerable moments. "Did you, um…"

"Can I come to your place? Just to chat or like if it's alright I'd ask to stay on the sofa for tonight but like you can tell me to fuck off. I don't want to impose, I just…" James is having one of those moments where he wishes he'd taken up smoking or some other vice that would give him something, anything, to do right now. But he's never even allowed himself that first drag, knowing it could become an obsessive habit or unhealthy coping mechanism immediately. "I know you're probably tired. Sorry."

"Everything alright?" Arthur asks again. James is very much a homebody a majority of the time. It's extremely unusual for him to go anywhere except straight to bed after a late shift.

"Fucking perfect." James laughs at himself, at the predicament he's in, at the fact that he's gone and caught feelings for his straight flatmate when he wasn't even aware he was interested in men.

The number of gay clubs he's been to with his mates on a night out, the number of men he's turned down at those clubs, the number of times he hesitated before doing so…His life is a twisted joke. "You mind if I crash at yours?"

"Course you can. Let's talk when I get home. Meet me there in half an hour?" Arthur is definitely typing again. James can hear it over the phone.

"You have no idea how much I love you right now. I owe you, Arthur." James hangs up and gives himself another five minutes leaning against the wall and letting himself spiral. He trusts Arthur, especially with this, and knowing he doesn't have to face his own flat tonight really helps.

Taking out his phone again after several grounding exercises, James finally answers August's message. He's probably asleep already, his companion for the night curled up beside him in the warmth of their flat. The image is nauseating.

James: *Staying at Arthur's tonight. Last minute. Haven't seen him and Karim for a few weeks. Be back tomorrow.*

James: *Glad the gig went well! I know it was an important one. Always proud of you, Augie.*

James calls a cab, too tired to walk to Arthur's flat at this hour. He's already been on his feet for a full shift, and now there's all this emotional shit to carry. While in the back of the cab, James types up his horoscopes for tomorrow's posts, or technically today's since it's well past midnight. They're due to his supervisor by seven in the morning and he doesn't see himself working on them at the Das-Anderson flat. His longer, weekly horoscope advice column was sent by Thursday afternoon, to be posted tomorrow, but the short posts he's allowed until the morning of.

Even by his own standards, today's horoscopes are a bit more bold and pointed:

Aquarius, you are more loved than you may ever know. Hold your loved ones close today and let them remind you.

Capricorn, you were right. Don't let it go to your head. Focus on the path still to come.

Virgo, you aren't appreciated nearly enough. Your friends rely on you and want you to know how much they care. You're their rock.

Leo, you pull them in like a moth to a flame. Like the shore to the sea. Your light is undeniable. Have pride in yourself. You've earned it.

He had to choose between Karim and Henri for Capricorn this round, but since Henri definitely reads these now, and he'll likely know what James is referring to, this is as close as James can get to texting him the same thing. Henri was right and James should've seen it all along. Blair always deserves a reminder that Henri (and everyone else) adores them, so hopefully that will be a nice Sunday thought for them. Arthur, the other Virgo of the group, isn't told often enough that he's the best support any of them could hope for. And August...

James can hardly blame him for bringing someone home. He gets a half dozen offers at every gig, girls (and even a few guys) flirting with him as soon as he's off the stage. So instead of being petty and snarky and rude, James aims for sincerity.

He's prouder of August than he can properly tell him. His perseverance, his determination to succeed as a singer, his kind heart through it all, even the stinging rejections and annoying roadblocks in the industry. August is an incredible man. James just wasn't aware until very recently that his feelings for August are more than platonic, made more apparent in contrast to his love for his other mates.

The thought of heading home and being very painfully conscious of what August is up to in his bedroom, maybe even hearing snippets before sneaking to his own room, it's just too much when James is already spiralling. Thank god for Arthur and Karim and their flat just a few streets away. He can hide out there until he has an idea of what he plans to do, until he's sure he can handle facing August again. The last thing he wants is to make August uncomfortable in his own home.

***

"So, that should keep you warm, I suppose." Arthur drops another blanket atop the pile of sheets and the pillow he's already laid on the sofa for James. "You good?"

"Actually, I was hoping we could talk?" James watches Arthur apprehensively, keeping his voice low so that he doesn't wake Karim in the other room. Karim teaches sixth form English Literature, so even if it's the weekend, he needs his sleep. "I know it's late, but I just - "

"It's fine." Arthur reassures him, setting a warm hand on his shoulder and guiding them both to sit. The sofa's not been transformed into a makeshift bed yet, so it's as good a place as any for whatever conversation he can tell James is bursting to have.

"So…" James sits beside Arthur, hunched forward with his elbows on his knees. He's not nervous around Arthur, but he's in quite a state at the moment. "You know in uni? Like early days?"

James pauses to clear his throat, trying to find how to ask what he desperately needs to understand. "You were straight until Karim came along, yeah? And I was wondering what that was like to go through, the realisation and the coming out, if you don't mind sharing."

"This is about August." Arthur lets his statement hang in the air without elaboration.

Maybe James should be surprised, but it seems it's been obvious to Arthur just like it had been to Henri. They're two of his oldest friends. Of course they noticed.

"You knew?" James turns his head to ask, staring at Arthur and searching for answers. There's more than one reason that Arthur was his first and only call tonight.

"I had a feeling. Recognised a few things, especially the past year or so." Arthur shrugs, leaning sideways on the sofa and supporting his head with one hand while his elbow rests against the back cushion. "And I was never straight, just repressed. Once Karim shocked my system, I looked back and a lot of things started making sense. I was always bi, I just sort of ignored it. Being out as a teenager wouldn't have been an option outside my immediate family, so I just dismissed those feelings and thoughts until I was ready. And when I met Karim,

I was in a safe environment and our connection broke through what was left of my internal walls."

"But I'm twenty five. Shouldn't I know by now? Even with whatever's going on, I don't know that anything's changed." James sits back against the sofa, mirroring Arthur's posture. Even as he says it, he knows it's not entirely true, because he wouldn't be having this crisis if what he was feeling for August was strictly platonic. "I don't think I've been actively hiding or anything like that, so shouldn't I have realised ages ago?"

"Not necessarily. It wasn't that I hadn't had crushes or been attracted to lads before Karim, he was just...undeniable. I met him and everything transformed." Arthur smiles, full of fond memories of life with his husband. Karim may have been his first gay relationship, but he was also Arthur's last. "I was so sure. I mean, it was so - you probably remember my panic and my gay crisis those first few weeks. You had to deal with it first hand, sharing the flat. And thank god for Henri. Not sure that I would've fallen so easily into my queer identity without his support."

"But you knew with Karim right away? It seemed like you did. And I've been living with August for almost two years." James gets the Karim thing. He's literally the most attractive human any of them have ever known, and that's just objectively true.

When Karim and Arthur met it was like lightning to Arthur's system, because Karim wasn't just fit, he wanted Arthur from that first moment and he wasn't shy about it. Hot and determined is a dangerous combination. Arthur never stood a chance. Undeniable seems an apt description for the way Karim entered Arthur's life. But James has known August for a while and he's only started to consciously think about the possibility of being interested in him since Henri's visit.

"Did something happen with August? Is that why you're not home?" Arthur drops his arm to sit up straighter, concern for James clear in his eyes.

43

"Not really, no." James sighs and runs his hands down his face. His body may be exhausted but his mind is wide awake. "Henri may have pointed some things out a few weeks ago. Gently, of course, but once it was in my head, I've sort of been spiralling. I brushed him off, but with time to think, he made some fair points. And then tonight…"

James stops to groan as those unsettling words pop into his mind in high definition, as if imprinted there by a cruel deity. "August texted me that he brought someone home after his gig and I felt…Henri even asked me what I would feel if that happened, because it came up in our conversation that I was glad when things ended with August's last girlfriend. At the time I told Henri he was daft, but he was right. I saw that text and it was like the world was crashing down. Don't know how I made it through my shift, if I'm honest. Was nearly sick thinking about going home, knowing that he…well."

"Couldn't face all that tonight?" Arthur gives him another understanding smile. Of all their friends, he certainly empathises the deepest with the situation that James is currently navigating.

Henri knew he was gay quite young, Blair was born as an angelic queer being who had no doubts at any age (and a family who always allowed them to be their spectacular self), and Karim realised he was bi at around fifteen without it being much of a crisis. Until now, Arthur's the only one of their friends who's come out during their time knowing each other.

"I don't know what to do. I don't even know what I'm feeling. Like, since when do I fancy lads? And August is my flatmate and he's straight and I can't tell him and make everything uncomfortable. He doesn't deserve that. He's done nothing wrong." James understands that he needs to keep his feelings to himself and figure out his sexuality crisis without ruining his friendship with August. But they share space, they have their daily routines, they spend a lot of time together. It won't be easy.

"If I'm being candid…I'm not entirely sure that's an accurate measure of the situation." Arthur messes up his hair, not meeting James's inquisitive gaze for the first time all night.

"You think I don't fancy him? I didn't think so either until Henri pointed it out, but now I'm pretty sure. It feels that way, even if it's turning my head." James imagines that unknowable feeling he couldn't name like one of those domino portraits: once the first piece fell it was inevitable, the picture becoming clearer with each toppled tile and the process unstoppable until the conclusion is reached.

Arthur waits to answer for almost an entire minute, studying James with a hand over his mouth and a furrowed brow. When he finally responds, scratching at his chin and still watching James carefully, it's with an unexpected suggestion. "I think you should ask him out."

"I should what?!" James laughs loudly before remembering Karim is asleep and throwing a palm across his now firmly shut lips to smother the noise. Once he's certain he has his volume under control, he finishes the thought. "Sorry, just, why the hell would I do that?"

"There's some things you need to figure out on your own, but that's my advice. Ask him out." Arthur shrugs as if it's a perfectly reasonable suggestion. Karim sleeps through almost anything so Arthur's not worried about waking him, even with James's bark of a laugh. "I'm glad to keep talking about your own identity and what being attracted to August means for you, but as far as what to do about your feelings, that's all I'm saying: Ask him out."

"There's no way. I don't know how to ask anyone out, least of all my heterosexual flatmate. I go out to the pubs, I pull sometimes, keep it all very casual, but like, August is someone I know. Someone I *live with*. I can't just - " James waves a hand in the air between them, letting the gesture finish his sentence.

What's he meant to do? Knock on August's bedroom door and give him his number in case he's keen?

"Yes, let's get back to you. Now that you're on board with this whole *feelings for August* situation, have you been thinking back on your adolescent gay crushes and watching coming out videos and taking gay quizzes online and listening to Troye Sivan?" Arthur teases.

James is taking all of this very well, even if he called Arthur in a panic in the middle of the night. It can be a lot to process, especially with James's tendency to hyperfixate to the point of dysfunction.

"There may have been a quiz or two." James mumbles, his entire face turning red at the admission. Is he really that predictable? "Maybe a few videos."

"And?" Arthur nudges James with his knee, waiting for his answer. He remembers taking those quizzes, typing desperately into google and finding whichever YouTuber's coming out video he hadn't watched yet until he heard an experience similar to his own. It had been extremely validating.

"Think I could be somewhere on the bisexual spectrum. Pansexual, maybe. Still attracted to women, that hasn't changed. The quizzes are a bit stupid but they helped me sort my thoughts." James picks at a nonexistent speck on his jeans.

The first few quizzes he took were mostly rubbish, but then he found one that really helped him examine his wills, won'ts, and wants, physically and romantically. Looking at his identity in that way was easier somehow, no complicated feelings or specific people to distract him. And the consensus was not a heterosexual one.

James is much more open than he'd really considered before. He's certainly not turned off by attractive men, or male bodies, or really any bodies. And the idea of dating a man or having sex with a man doesn't bother him at all. There's no gender or expression he's not attracted to when he earnestly thinks about it, his own body having reacted to all the different sexual content he'd searched the last

46

several days in an attempt to find clarity. Except feet. Definitely no foot fetish.

But allowing himself to watch gay porn without laughing it off or assuming it wasn't for him was a new experience. He let his hands wander, let his mind imagine, let his eyes devour, and he got off to the idea of sex with a man without issue. More than once. "I'm fine with the idea of being queer, I've just never known I might be. So like, my crisis hasn't been as much internalised homophobia as it is feeling incredibly stupid for not realising all these years."

"You realise you had a crush on Blair when you first met?" Arthur waits for James to splutter and flush, because yes, he had realised that, but how had Arthur known and he didn't?

"Only for about ten minutes before we actually knew each other, so you can put away that smirk." James shoves Arthur's shoulder while he laughs, settling back into his own side of the sofa with a yawn. "They're gorgeous, obviously. I'm not ashamed of that."

"You certainly have a type. Tall, with dark curls and a gorgeous smile. And the eyes. They've both got great eyes." Arthur doesn't seem phased in the slightest by this conversation, but James is still swirling inside. The thought spirals don't just disappear all at once, even if he's feeling much better now than he was an hour ago.

"Think I've had at least a handful of crushes on lads growing up, a few times I was definitely interested, just didn't recognise it for what it was. Don't know that I would've figured out about August either until Henri pointed it out." James stifles another yawn.

Talking to Arthur is helping more than anything else so far. Arthur understands and he's very much a judgement free space when it comes to matters of latent queer identity. "Suppose you think I'm a coward, running away to hide here because my crush has someone over and I'm in my feelings about it."

"Of course I don't think you're a coward. You're trying to figure yourself out. You don't have to face everything all at once." Arthur leans forward to set his hand on James's knee, giving it a squeeze before sitting back. "You're welcome here whenever you need space."

"Think I might actually be able to sleep for a few hours, if you're sure about me staying. Thanks for the chat and being nice about it and all that." James rubs the exhaustion from his eyes. He isn't sure what time it is, but it's late. Very late. And it's been a long night. "I didn't know it was so obvious to everyone. I promise I had no clue."

"I figured you'd come to me when the time was right." Arthur gives James another smile and stands up from the sofa, ready to let them both rest after a much needed talk. "Karim and I might be sleeping in tomorrow, so if you wake up before us, help yourself to whatever you need. Coffee, shower, food, our home is yours, alright?"

"You're genuinely the best. Tell Karim thank you when you wake him up. His home, too." James gives Arthur a brief wave goodnight and waits for him to disappear into the bedroom before sliding out of his jeans and shirt to sleep in his pants. This won't be the first time he's down to his birthday suit in the same flat as these two.

It takes James a few minutes to get the sheets and pillows arranged, but luckily Arthur is very particular about his furniture and Karim encourages his attention to detail, so the sofa is extremely comfortable, all things considered. The fact that two of his best mates are feet away in case anything happens tonight also bestows a blessed calm that settles over James in the dark. He's safe here.

James falls asleep thinking of August, the way his eyes sparkle when he's excited, the scar on his cheek that he has a new story for every time someone asks, the million pound grin that he flashes at the audience between sets, how he smells of fresh laundry when they're together at home, the way James feels so easy in August's presence.

With a sigh, James pulls the sheets over his head and lets his mind wander further, thinking about the possibility of a date, running his hands through that curly hair, leaning in for a kiss goodnight. Arthur's suggestion of asking August out enters the thought spiral, but slower, floating, like a melody on the wind. Maybe, just maybe...

CHAPTER TWO

James doesn't act on his feelings for August for another week. Since his night spent at Arthur's, he's been much more alright with everything. He's accepted he's not in any way straight and he's tried to proceed as usual with August, not ready to do anything quite yet, or maybe ever, at least not with his flatmate. James has always been cautious, not one to make rash decisions or be impulsive. If he does act on his feelings it won't be by accident.

He hasn't come out to anyone yet. James still isn't sure what he would even come out as. Henri hasn't pressured him, but James is positive he saw the horoscope for Capricorn that he posted that night and decided to give him space around the topic. Arthur hasn't brought it up either, but he's started sending James queer memes and tiktoks, even more than usual. It's like Arthur knows he can share that side of himself with James more completely now.

It's interesting how this understanding of himself started as a spiral and turned into a new sort of community. James has never felt outside of his friendships or anything like that. But now he knows what it is to realise he's queer, to wake up one day and understand that even though he's always been told he's right handed, he's actually a leftie (which in his case is literally true). Though to follow that metaphor, he's some variety of ambidextrous. He'd mentioned to Arthur that he's somewhere in the multi-gender attraction spectrum, and with another week to think about it, he's even more sure of that.

James has been reflecting deeper the last few days. He's past the initial panic and he's trying to maintain a semblance of normalcy in his flat despite his...whatever it is (he's determined to stop calling it a crush). While getting through his regular days of work and writing and all the rest, James has been realising some of those things that his queer friends have told him about from their own experience with identity exploration.

He's definitely had interest in men before and just didn't understand it for what it was. When James thinks back to the few physically intimate queer experiences he's had, the reason they didn't do anything for him is that those people just weren't his type.

Not that James has only one type, but he does have preferences. He's always favoured people with brown hair, regardless of gender. Curly hair is a plus, as Arthur teased him about. And there's something about specific voices that also draw him in, from August's warm tenor to James's most recent ex, Tori, and her tinkling laugh. It's not only physical features that play a role in his attraction, which is a piece of the puzzle he'd underestimated.

Recognising how scent and sound and touch compound his attraction to someone helped James see that his sexuality is so much more than heterosexual. He would've thought after years of being mates with all queer people (as Henri had helpfully pointed out) he would know that experiencing attraction is multi-faceted and nuanced. But it's different understanding it for himself, from the inside of the queer experience rather than as an ally.

It's been just over a week since August brought someone home and James couldn't stomach it. A week of their usual afternoon chats and trying not to stare too deep or linger when their hands touch. A week of being hyper aware of his behaviour, noticing his sweaty palms when August wanders around without a shirt and the dreams that have started to come almost every night. Dirty, occasionally, but more often than not the dreams are about their life as James knows it, just shifted. Holding hands while they chill on the sofa, kissing against the fridge while one of them cooks on a Sunday afternoon, sleeping together for the few hours that their schedules align and spooning the entire time.

James hasn't forgotten Arthur's suggestion, but he didn't seriously consider it until yesterday. They'd had their usual chat around the table, and James had a few extra hours before work, so they decided to order in and share a meal before he headed to the pub for his shift and August got ready for bed ahead of an early morning at the cafe.

Just a typical quiet evening at the flat together. They ordered Nandos and settled into the sofa with a few beers and watched the first thing they could agree to on Netflix.

August fell asleep about halfway through the film. Well fed and tired from work, he dozed off, snoring softly with his shining curls fanned out around his head. James tried to wake him up, to get him to go nap properly in his bed, but August refused, instead shoving James into the corner of the sofa, fitting himself into James's space, and using him as a pillow. August was asleep again in under a minute, face resting against James's chest, and James wasn't about to refuse. This was his happiest moment in recent memory.

James let the film play out, trying his best not to move and disturb August. He didn't watch a single moment of what was on the screen, instead focusing on the beautiful soul attached to his front. August had been the one to initiate the cuddling, and James doesn't want to read too much into it because he knows it doesn't have to mean anything.

But here he is, the morning after being used as a nap cushion, starting his day by tidying up the flat while August is at work. Not that there's much to tidy. There never is. Lacking a sufficient distraction, James can't stop glancing at that spot on the sofa and thinking about it. Obsessing, but not in a self destructive way for once.

There's something about such a simple night, a bit of comfort and a quiet evening together, that has James ready to take Arthur's advice. He's thought it through considerably since the moment it was suggested, and as of last night, it doesn't seem quite so ludicrous.

August's smile sparkles a bit brighter for him. He leans on James for emotional support, even when he has other options. James has also realised that he isn't the only one whose touch lingers sometimes, even if he'd always brushed it off as insignificant before.

Maybe August is in a similar situation. James doesn't know if August realises he might have non platonic feelings in return, but now that

James is aware of the potential, he could see it. It's not completely out of the realm of possibility. Cautious, but more optimistic than he had been before last night, James makes a decision.

James: How's work, sleepyhead?
August: /yawning cat gif/
August: Still tired, but it's been alright.
August: Thursdays aren't so bad. Not as busy as the weekend crowd.
August: And Tiff's here now so we're having fun between customers.
James: What's the drink of the day?
August: Lavender honeycomb latte /purple heart emoji; bee emoji; honeypot emoji/
James: Your idea?
August: How'd you know?
James: Sweet, bougie, and smells incredible? It's August Alberto Lopes in a cup.
August: Keep throwing out my middle name, I'll think you're being serious.
James: Maybe I am.
James: Let me know when you're on break? Got something I want to run by you.
August: /saluting emoji/
August: I'll get a break before Grant leaves, so not much longer.

An hour later, James gets a text confirming August is on his break, followed by a selfie in the late morning sun. It would appear that he took his break outside, likely to take advantage of the rare, beaming sunshine. August is smiling beneath his sunglasses, hair tousled and bright and perfect. James bites his bottom lip, grinning at the image and the warmth that floods his chest. It's now or never, he supposes.

Riding that wave of inexplicable hope, James brings his phone to his ear and waits.

The call rings three times before August answers, his tone surprised. James doesn't usually call him, especially because they'll literally be sitting around their kitchen table together in a few hours. A text accomplishes anything immediate that can't wait until they see one another, so this is obviously something different.

"Hey, man, what's up?" August's voice is so comforting from the first note, and James can't believe he didn't notice his feelings for so long. Time wasted, but he can't dwell on that right now.

"I sort of have a question for you." James stands facing the window in their living room, looking out at the alley and wondering if there's a world where someday he gets a view of a park or even a garden to call his own. His mind tends to wander when he's nervous but he needs to focus. "You have a few to chat? Don't want to disrupt your break."

"It's cool. Tiff's got it handled and she still has Grant in case it picks up." August sounds like he's shrugging off James's hesitancy, like it's actually no big deal for James to be calling him like this. That might change once he hears why James rang. "Something wrong at the flat?"

"No, nothing like that." James laughs quietly, looking down at his feet on the old wood floor and grinning, his heart fluttering in anticipation. He knows this feeling, and it's validating to keep receiving confirmation that this part of him is real, as new as it seems.

Here goes nothing. "I was actually wondering if I could take you out?"

August waits approximately three seconds to reply, and in those three seconds James's breakfast lurches in his throat, his hands start shaking, and his vision goes blurry. He can't remember being this nervous since he was a teenager. It's like having his first crush all over again.

"Oh, like you want to get a drink tonight? It'd have to be early, since I work at five thirty again tomorrow." August sounds like he's fidgeting with something. The neck of his henley, if James had to guess, but his voice has definitely taken on a nervous undercurrent. "You could've just texted me." He laughs a bit, the sound like warm marmalade that James can nearly taste.

"No - I mean sure, we can if you want - but I was actually hoping, like - " James pauses and takes a deep breath. He should've been more specific, made it clear that he's not talking about two mates hanging out. "I'd make us a reservation, take you out for dinner somewhere special where we'd dress smart and you'd order one of your healthy vegan things and there would be candles and flowers and a waiter who seems too posh to be serving us."

August is silent again, and James swears he can hear his brain putting the gay puzzle pieces together. To be fair to August, James hasn't made the clearest of offers or given any prior warning about this conversation. James has had weeks to put together his thoughts on the matter, so he shouldn't expect August to figure out a response at the speed of sound. But then - "A date. You want to take me on a date?"

"Yes, that." James's shoulders are so high they're hiding his earrings, delicate little hoops he's worn since his first year of uni. "So, erm…thoughts?"

"I'm…confused?" August sounds it, his voice going up and James can identify the noise of him scratching a hand through his curls. The fact he knows August's habits so intimately maybe should've clued him in to his interest earlier.

"You can say no!" James hurries to add. He's doing a very shit job of asking August out. It was always going to be awkward, but whatever charm he usually employs has apparently evaporated. "I just, um…" He has no idea how he intended to finish that sentence.

"Do you, like…do you want to date me?" August's voice doesn't sound upset or angry, and James is trying to decipher his answer before it's given, like a terrible game of *Clue*. Is there any chance he's considering accepting James's invitation?

"I think I do, yes. You're sort of incredible, you know? But you can absolutely tell me no and I'll never mention it again. I don't want to make you upset or uncomfortable or anything like that." James starts chewing on his lower lip nervously. August hasn't cursed him out, which is something.

"Why did you call instead of asking me literally anytime that we're home together?" August wonders aloud, in his usual tone. It's a fair question. James did employ this method for a reason, though.

"I didn't want you to feel pressured to say yes just because I was standing in front of you. Situation's different since we're flatmates. And this way if you hate the idea, or hate me for fancying you, we can just drop it and keep on as we were." James sighs through a heavy breath before adding, "And I'm bricking it. Didn't think I could work up the nerve with you looking at me with those puppy eyes while I tried to be brave and tell you that I…that you…so, yeah."

For a writer, sometimes he feels the failure of words like a physical ailment, the way they slip through his grasp like water through a sieve while he aches for relief. James has practised every version of a declaration of emotion through his writing only to have *that* be how he admits to August that he has feelings for him. Brilliant.

"So… when's the date?" August finally asks after letting James stew in his anxiety for another several moments.

That wasn't a no.

"Are you saying yes?" James hears his voice break and wishes he were like one of the smooth, sweet talking heroes in a period romance. How can he expect August to want him when he can barely get a coherent thought out?

"Sure. I've never, like, dated a guy before, but first time for everything." August laughs again, but James knows it's not at him. Maybe he's feeling a little nervous too? That sounded like his nervous laugh. Hopefully nervous for potentially liking James reasons and not because he's uncomfortable.

"So when's the date?" August repeats, since James still hasn't answered. He should probably do that, seeing as he's received the best response he could've hoped for.

"Monday night? It's my night off at the pub and I was hoping you could maybe see about going in later on Tuesday since it's a slower day at the cafe?" James thought about this for the entire hour between texting August and giving him a call. Monday made the most sense. "And if it goes terribly, I can stay at Arthur and Karim's and you can have the flat until you're alright with me coming by again."

"I'm not kicking you out of the flat, James." August's voice is suddenly much firmer than it has been for the rest of the conversation. He sounds offended for some reason. "There's nothing wrong with you asking me on a date. You're being very respectful about it and you're definitely not forcing anything on me. I'm agreeing because I want to. Oh, and like," August's voice immediately gets all soft again. Quieter. "Is this you coming out to me? *Sorry,* I think maybe I wasn't supposed to say it like that."

"No, you're completely fine! Brilliant, actually. I don't even know what I am. No labels to share yet, but maybe soon." James is so glad he decided to do this over the phone. There's something about the physical space between them that's letting him admit more than he's ready to in person. This could turn into an entirely different conversation that they don't really have time for while August is on his break. "I just…fancy you."

There's another pause on August's end and James hopes it's alright to confirm what he's been dancing around. He likes August and now he's told him. He has formally, out loud, said the words. It's a huge step in a direction. Hopefully a positive one.

"Monday? Text me the details and I'll add it to my schedule, make sure I have an outfit ready. I'll ask Grant and Tiff if we can swap hours on Tuesday, just in case." August is back to sounding like his usual warm self, as if it's any other Thursday morning. James hopes it's a good sign that the only time he seemed offended during the call was when James was worried that August might want him to stay out of the flat. That seems alright? They'll be alright?

"Yes, definitely. You can, um…back to work." James can't believe he's made it through this conversation. "And could we just be ourselves until Monday? Chat over pastries and share our space as usual? I don't want to ruin, like, us?"

"If that's what you want." August yawns, and James is reminded of last night all over again. The smell of his shampoo, the warmth of August on his chest, the pleasant feeling of having him so close. He'd trusted James on some base level to sleep on him like that on purpose. "You don't have to sound so scared, Jay. It's just a date. Worst case we have a night out together and leave it at that."

"Right. Of course you're right." James can't believe how calm August is being about all this. Especially with his anxiety, he seems to be taking this news and their upcoming date in his stride. He's acting as if he's not surprised, but James knows he is. "I'll see you in a bit then. At home."

"I'll bring you an almond croissant or two. Accidentally made a double batch this morning so there's plenty and I know they're one of your favourites. Always stealing them before I can even finish opening the box. I would usually surprise you, but it seems we've hit our surprise quota for the day, eh?" August sounds like he's teasing? Flirting?

James isn't sure he can handle flirting from August. He never let himself think that far. Fuck.

Voice cracking once again, James expresses his gratitude and ends the call before he can embarrass himself further.

"Oh my god. Oh my fucking god. Jesus Mary and Joseph." James drops the phone on the sofa beside himself and stares out at the building across from theirs, hands in his hair while he replays the conversation over and over and over and over and over. He spends the time until August gets home pacing and worrying and tidying and thinking then overthinking. But August said yes and James eventually remembers to text him the details of their date after calling the restaurant to confirm a reservation for two next Monday evening.

He has a date with August. And he has no idea how he made that happen.

***

James: I'm only saying this once and I'm not ready for questions but I have something to share and it's not like I'm hiding it but I'm still not sure what it means or how I feel about everything. But it seems weird not to tell you all because then it would feel like lying so this is me telling you and please be normal about it.
Blair: James???
Karim: He said no questions. You've already failed.
Blair: He also said to be normal and I've no idea how to do that.
Karim: Neither do I, to be fair.
Henri: Oh. /side eye emoji/
Arthur: OH. OKAY THEN.
James: I haven't even told you yet.
Blair: I'm being so normal and respecting that side eye from Hen without asking questions.
Arthur: BUT I KNOW ALREADY AND IM SCREAMING
Karim: He's not. He's just grinning at his phone and typing and deleting over and over.
Karim: Arthur's so cute /heart eye emoji/
Henri: ...do I also know?
James: I haven't even told most of you what's going on?
James: And yes, you and Arthur both sort of know. Sigh.
Blair: Sorry, yes, go ahead.
Blair: Wait what does Henri already know?

Blair: /selfie with William at the park/
Blair: William is waiting patiently.
Henri: His parents are waiting less patiently
James: I swear to god how am I meant to tell you now? The way you all carry on /eye roll emoji/
Arthur: ITS FINE ITS COMPLETELY FINE WE ARE HERE AND READY TO BE SUPPORTIVE
Arthur: RIGHT EVERYONE??
Karim: Babe, maybe put away the all caps.
Arthur: Sorry. I will type with my inside voice.
James: So as I was saying…
James: I've asked August on a date and it's tomorrow night and he's said yes and I still don't understand why he's agreed because I stumbled my way through the asking but it's a thing that's happening. I'm taking him to dinner and etc.
Blair: August as in Lopes?
Blair: The outrageously handsome Canadian giant that you live with?
Arthur: Excuse me, what is included in the etc?
Karim: What part of no questions??
Karim: James wants to tell us about his gay date, but he doesn't want us to contribute to the spiral by making it into a whole thing.
James: Karim is correct.
Blair: …if we can't ask questions, is Junior allowed?
James: He can't even speak yet.
Blair: I'll ask for him. Like a translator.
Henri: Proud of you, Jay!
Arthur: IM SO EXCITED FOR YOU
Karim: Babe.
Arthur: Sorry. Again.
James: I don't want this to be a big deal. Like it is because he's my flatmate and he's a lad and all that but like it's just a date, yeah? I don't even know if it means anything yet and it might be shit.
Henri: It won't be shit. I know you and you've definitely planned it all out.
Arthur: He's not just some random person out in the world. I know you don't want it to be a big thing but…
James: I know. Believe me, I know.

Blair: Did you want to meet us for an early dinner? We could go after Junior's had his nap? We're leaving the park in a minute.
Karim: Are we invited?
James: Only on the condition that none of you bring it up or ask any questions. If I'm feeling ready to talk about it I will but I'm not there yet.
Henri: Am I allowed a cuddle? Just a quick like brotherly acceptance moment.
James: I'll allow that, yes. But please let's just have a nice meal because I don't need to obsess over this any more than I already am.
Arthur: We can do that. I also request a hug in advance, but that's up to you.
James: Each of you is allowed exactly one hug.
James: Except Junior. He's allowed infinity. Obviously.
Henri: I'll text you when he's up from his nap and we can all head to that place with the sandwiches.
Karim: Ah, yes, the only place that fits that description.
Henri: Fuck off you know where I mean
Karim: /painted nails emoji/
Arthur: See you then /red heart emoji; rainbow emoji/

***

August has been remarkably normal since James asked him out. Maybe James shouldn't be surprised since he'd been the one who asked for that to be the case and August is clearly respecting his wishes. But there hasn't been a single moment of awkwardness or any hint that August is uncomfortable living with James now that he knows James has feelings for him. They both go to work as usual, chat between shifts, and revolve around the flat like nothing's changed.

But now it's almost time for their date, and James might actually have some sort of cardiac event if he doesn't find a way to calm down, and soon. August should be home from work any minute. With their date planned in a few hours, instead of their usual catch up around the kitchen table, they'll be getting ready in their separate rooms and then heading out. Which means this is really happening.

James has already prepared his horoscopes for tomorrow, but he's waiting to send them until he knows how the date goes. Since August still reads them, and has no idea that James writes them, he either wants to subtly reveal his hand via tomorrow's post or, assuming he's told August by then, choose a ridiculous sappy post that's going to make him melt. But he has to wait until after the date to know which to submit. And both options are predicated on the assumption the date goes well, which is, to be fair, a huge assumption.

James is just putting away his folded laundry when August's singing reaches his ears, a rendition of Fleetwood Mac's *Everywhere,* and James's nerves aren't going anywhere soon. That's one of his favourite songs and hearing August serenade him with his perfect voice as he slides into their flat with a grin is almost too much when James is already on edge.

"Hey, man." August closes the door and toes off his shoes.

James is still adjusting to his Canadian slang years into living together, so different from back in Ireland or what he's surrounded by here in London. He knows that August didn't mean anything by it, but his greeting did sound very platonic. Almost intentionally so. Which they are, technically, so it shouldn't sting like it does. But James is fine and definitely not overthinking that simple phrase.

"Work was good?" James confirms, glad to see that August still brought home a few treats to share, even if they won't be eating them straight away. Maybe dessert later?

"Work was great. Mondays are always fun when that knitting group comes by for a few hours. They're working on socks this week." August sidles up to James, and if they weren't about to go on a date he probably wouldn't think too much of it. But they are, and August is in his space and it's on purpose. So maybe not so platonic...

James can't decide if the mixed signals are just his own brain or if August might be unsure of how to act now that it's all very real.

"Did you - I figured I'd let you shower first since I won't take very long to get ready - not that you need to shower! You can definitely just go like this, I don't mind." James glances up to catch his eye because August is significantly taller than him. Those damn Canadian hockey genes. Though apparently August's parents are Welsh and Portuguese originally, so maybe he's just a human tree regardless of nationality.

"A shower sounds perfect. And I'm definitely getting dressed up for tonight." August surprises James by pulling him into a hug, his arms strong and warm around James's back. James falters, hugging August back a moment too late. It's not that they've never hugged before, he's just…adjusting. "I don't really get to do the whole dinner and a night out with like actual outfits and all that. I'm taking advantage. Have to impress my date somehow."

"You already do." James doesn't dare break the hug. It's far too pleasant. August smells of espresso and butter and his cologne that he charges in the moonlight. James tries not to inhale too deeply, or at least keep it from being obvious while considering the possibility of an August scented candle, and maybe he's literally lost his mind to even consider wanting one.

"I'm off to clean up, then." August steps away from the hug, James's hands lingering on his waist even as he goes. It's nice to be in August's arms, comfortable and familiar, and James's breathing has settled for the first time since waking up. He tries not to think too hard about that and what could happen if tonight changes everything between them.

James lets August walk almost all the way across the room before stopping him with the question he has to ask. "Are you sure? I know you've said yes, I just…you don't have to. I won't be upset if you've changed your mind."

"I'm very sure." August looks at James over his shoulder with that sunshine smile, as easy as ever. "Looking forward to it."

"But you don't even like me. Not like…you know." He leaves off the *like I like you* for his own sake. He's too nervous to get into that now. James runs a hand through his hair, glad he'll be redoing his quiff because it's been destroyed throughout the day while he worried at it.

"Isn't that what dates are for? To find out if you like someone? We'll just have to wait and find out together." August leaves James with that, disappearing into the bathroom and starting to sing again as the sound of the flowing tap joins in.

"Right." James answers the empty air, still standing where August left him. He really needs to get a grip and pull himself together if he has any chance of making this a successful evening.

Hiding away in his room until August finishes with the shower, James calls Arthur for a pep talk, incredibly grateful that he picks up. He's always going to need his mates, and he's exceptionally lucky that they're some of the best people in the world. It takes a few minutes, but Arthur talks him off the proverbial cliff, reminding him it's just a date and he's thought about essentially every possibility and if it all goes wrong he can always stay with Arthur and Karim while he figures out what's next.

Knowing there's a back up plan to the back up plan helps calm his intrusive thoughts and by the time he's ready for his own shower, James is breathing soundly and his mind is calm. He's made his choice and soon enough he's going to find out if it was the right one.

After his chat with Arthur, James gets a string of texts from Henri, all supportive and proud, like an older brother sending love before a big game or an important meeting or something. He's absolutely lovely and James types him a short novel about how grateful he is that Henri had that first awkward conversation with him, especially when he was so determined not to have it. James isn't sure how long it would've taken him to realise his feelings if Henri hadn't read his horoscopes and brought it up.

Stepping into the shower, James can tell that August is nervous, hopefully for good reasons. August has used practically every product he owns, the room coated in his intoxicating smell. James almost feels bad mingling it with his own, but then he remembers how that could become a very different process in the future if tonight goes well and he spends his shower distracted by what could be and only remembers to exfoliate with a minute of hot water to spare.

He's never been this anxious for a date in his life. Most of his dates are much more casual, and even more often, he meets someone at the pub or on an app and they hurry their way through the pleasantries to get to shagging, moving on with their lives before it could get to the point of involving feelings. He's had relationships, but nothing serious, not really.

But if this is *something* with August, if they start dating, it won't be casual. Their lives are already too intertwined for any alternative.

***

"James, you look…" August whistles, giving James an appraising look and if James isn't imagining things, he's flushing slightly. Interesting.

"Yeah? Been told I clean up nice." James shrugs, but then he laughs and gives a twirl, August laughing along and catching his arm in the space near their front door.

James is feeling much more confident after talking to both Arthur and Henri, and the picture of William giving him a thumbs up (with Blair's help of course) warmed his entire soul before he stepped out of his room to start their date. The fact Karim hasn't texted him is definitely due to his commitment to *not make it a big deal* and James appreciates him respecting that boundary. That's why tomorrow he'll be the first person to get all the dirtiest details that James is ready to share. Karim's a fucking vault.

"Nice? James, I'm questioning my entire existence." August drops James's elbow and gives a twirl of his own. He's gorgeous and James briefly considers forgetting the date and just snogging him right here, right now. "You like the suit?"

With a surge of excitement, James reaches out, tugging August forward by the lapels until they're standing flush and throwing them both clearly past the boundary of platonic interaction. He can hear August's breath catch before he relaxes against James, eyes wide and sparkling. Not being pushed away in disgust is a good sign.

"Suppose you look alright." James teases, letting his hands flatten across August's chest until they reach his shoulders, giving them a squeeze.

August is wearing a charcoal suit over a pitch black shirt, his hair soft and shining around his perfect face. Yes, James has decided it's perfect. He literally can't find a flaw. Even his cheek scar makes him more attractive somehow, and his eyes are like amber, glowing when he smiles.

Their outfits complement each other well, James's own black suit and powder blue shirt showcasing his stormy blue eyes. Apparently so, anyway. Like his dad, James is colour blind, so he always has to check with someone else when purchasing clothes to make sure they actually are the colour he thinks they are. But inability to evaluate colour aside, James is enchanted by August in formal attire, excited to have a posh night together and see where it leads.

"So." August smiles down at his shoes and clears his throat, hand in front of his mouth while trying to hide his smile. Maybe James still has a bit of that charm that gets him both in and out of trouble. "Should we head out?"

"Ride will be here in a minute, but first - wait here." James holds a hand up to ask August to stay put before hurrying back to his room and grabbing the ridiculous little gift he'd found. He's always thought flowers were the thing for a first date, but August doesn't like them. Did he spend too much time choosing an appropriate alternative? Possibly. But if he's doing this, if he's romancing August, he's doing it properly.

With a patience to be admired, August waits obediently until James returns, lighting up when he sees the handheld potted plant that James offers to him. August's reaction is pure, unexpected joy. "A philodendron?"

"For your windowsill. You don't fancy cut flowers, and this one has heart shaped leaves. Found it at the market." James swallows down his nerves as their hands graze, August's delicate fingers definitely taking a moment beyond what's necessary to shift the small ceramic pot from James's grasp.

"This is so - James, you're such a romantic. No one's ever brought me something on a date." August finds James's gaze again to give him a shy smile. His eyes are softer now, warm and wide open. "Do we have time for me to go get it settled in my room?"

"I factored it in, yes." James smirks, secretly triumphant in his deduction skills. He'd figured that August would immediately need to take his new green child and introduce it to its friends. How did he ever think he wasn't infatuated with this wonderful man? "Go on then. I'll wait here."

August holds the plant in both of his palms, walking back into his bedroom while James watches on with a grin. Yes, he certainly is a romantic. And now that the date's started he's in his element. He can woo. He can romance. He can charm. Especially someone as lovely and hilarious and easy going as August. They already know they have many, many things in common. This might even be fun.

***

"Are you sure we're meant to be here?" August whispers across the table to James, the two of them just sitting down after being led to their reserved table by the host.

"Probably not, but shhhh." James winks at August then stares down at his menu, already knowing what he's planning to order because he's researched their entire seasonal menu ahead of time. He didn't want to be distracted with something as inane as a menu when he should be focusing on his date.

"I've never been anywhere this nice." August is ignoring the (simple yet beautiful) tablescape and instead looking at James, his face holding an expression that James can't decipher. He knows August extremely well, but not in this context.

"Too much?" James asks, worried that he's overdone it and should've planned for something simpler. They're both fairly regular guys. A place like this definitely warrants a special occasion and it's well above their usual price range. But James had wanted this to be that special occasion, to show August that he was invested in playing his hand and going all out, especially if this was his only chance.

"Not too much at all. It's just…" August runs his fingers through his hair and glances around at the restaurant. There's mood lighting and candles and live music from somewhere distant and across the way there's spotless windows overlooking the city. "I'm adjusting and you're seeing it in real time. Never had someone be like…romantic for me. That's always been my job, but."

August tilts his head left and right, as if deciding. Looking up at James beneath his lashes, he admits, "I like it."

"Yeah?" James may have his menu in hand, but his focus is 100% on August. "That was the goal, sweetheart."

August flushes and looks away from James then gives him a very heated look. James has never used a pet name for August before, but it felt nice. He could get used to spoiling August, especially if it makes him stare at James like that, like he's waiting for more, *wanting* more.

"Do you think - nevermind." August picks up his menu again hurriedly, almost dropping it to the floor before recovering the movement.

"Something wrong?" James asks, setting down his own menu rather than pretending to peruse the starters so that August knows he has his full attention.

"I was just wondering if you would order for me?" August flushes deeper until he's maroon, pulling his bottom lip into his mouth and waiting for James's answer with wide eyes. Such a sweet, sensitive soul, as if he's worried that James would laugh at the request.

"Be happy to." James reaches his hand across the table, palm up, hoping that August might take it. It'd be the first truly non platonic touch they've shared, and he wants to see if August will accept the opportunity.

August considers for only a moment before setting his hand atop James's and letting out seemingly all the air in his lungs. James holds on carefully, rubbing his thumb across the top of August's hand and hoping he can calm some of August's anxiety. He knew he'd been nervous earlier, but this is the first glimpse of it he's had since their evening started. "Practically memorised the menu. Let me take care of it, yeah?"

Let me take care of you is implied, but it's far too soon for something so bold.

"Thanks. I was just thinking…never tried that either. Letting someone else sort of run the show." August stares at their hands resting together on the table, looking equal parts happy and conflicted. Adjusting, as he'd told James a minute before. "But I trust you."

Which James knows. And he trusts August, too. He trusted August not to laugh at him for asking him out, or making things awkward if tonight didn't end anywhere new. How lucky is James that his first queer date is with someone as generous and kind as August? There's hardly anyone who could say the same.

"Can I ask you a question?" James is glad they haven't been interrupted to order just yet. It's likely due to it being a slow Monday night at the restaurant, but he's appreciating their moment alone. They both need it.

August tilts his head, considers for a moment, then nods. He's not usually so quiet, but James doesn't think he's upset. Maybe he's overwhelmed. It's a lot to take in. James has had weeks to process how he feels, and if August is maybe feeling something too, it's much newer for him.

"Why did you say yes?" James watches August carefully as he raises his eyes, a soft, sad sort of smile tilting his lips. He doesn't answer right away, but James knows he will, so he waits patiently, electrified by something as simple as their hands held together. It's lovely to have August in his grasp. James lets them sit in the quiet of their space, the ambient noise preserving their privacy from the other patrons.

"Because when you asked me out, my heart fell through the floor, and I knew that had to mean something." August holds James's stare as the sincerity of his answer hits James like a wall. "Everything turned upside down, but it felt like my world was finally upright after a life spent on a diagonal. You asked and everything changed in an instant, like a part of me was knocking at the front door, waiting to be let in."

"Oh." James might have to give up writing. August is far better with words. He's been spiralling for weeks, but August managed to hold a phone conversation with James while his identity transformed from within. He's remarkable.

"Sorry." August mumbles, taking his hand back and staring across at the windows again. They can't see much of the view from their table, but it's still nice. James wonders what sort of view August prefers, what countryside they could explore together, what holidays they could take, what adventures they could share.

"Please, don't apologise." James has never been more positive that he's falling for someone. *Undeniable*, as Arthur had said about Karim. James hasn't been the only one figuring this out. He's not alone. August is right here with him, physically, emotionally, on the same roller coaster of discovery. "That's the most wonderful thing anyone's ever said to me."

"It's not only that I'm nervous, because I'm actually really excited about this and I've been trying to play it cool all weekend." August readjusts in his seat and fusses with his shirt cuffs. They're both fidgety when distracted or really any mood above baseline. "I'm learning a lot about myself by the minute, but I'm really happy."

"Overwhelmed?" James asks, laughing softly, glad to see August return his smile. "This is all completely new for me too. The only thing I know for sure is that this is exactly where I want to be and who I want to be here with. As long as you feel the same, I think we'll figure it out."

They move past the discussion with a shared smile, James asking August about his wine preferences before their server comes by because the two of them don't actually drink wine together. They usually have beer at the pub and at home, shots if they're at the club, but they're enjoying a nice meal in a posh restaurant and James can splurge. Thanks to his side job, the same one that somehow ended them here, he can afford to give them a posh evening, and he can't think of a better way to spend that investment.

James orders them a full-bodied bordeaux and a starter to share, with August's compliments on his choices. They chat through their meal, as easy as always, the air cleared of any hesitation before the first glass of wine reaches the table. It's sweet and romantic and

72

something like a dream. James could float away if August didn't keep reaching for him across the table, like grasping James's hand is the best way to keep them both grounded as they find their way through the evening.

***

James: :) :) :)
Arthur: :)
Karim: :)
Blair: :)
Henri: :)
James: :) :) :) :) :)

***

James signals for a cab once they're outside of the restaurant. Ever the gentleman, he opens the door to help August inside with a hand on the small of his back, sliding in beside him and giving the driver their next address.

"We're not going home?" August looks at James with an adorably scrunched forehead. Did he really think James would end their evening so early?

"Hardly." James knocks his shoulder against August's and cracks a devious smile. "We've had the romance. Now it's time for a bit of fun."

"Oh, that's…" August might think he's being subtle, but he scans from James's eyes to his lips, down his chest to his lap, and then back to his face with his mouth slightly open. "I like fun."

"Thought so." James gives August an appraisal of his own, noting his wide eyes and the way he leans into James's space. His interest is withheld, but it's there.

Dinner went exceptionally well. There'd been flirting and jokes far too rude for their surroundings and the occasional foot brush beneath the table. What James has planned next will be an intense vibe shift, but hopefully August is into it.

"James?" August turns away from the window where he'd been people watching, this time staring at the vacant middle seat as he says his name with an impossibly soft voice. James is fairly sure he knows what August wants.

There's a respectable amount of room between them, so James presses their knees together before sliding his fingers to intertwine with August's, holding his hand atop the seat. August grins then looks up at him and sighs. He looks happy.

"I'll give you three guesses for where we're going and if you guess right you get a prize." James can't stop staring. August is a lot to take in even on a standard day, but tonight he's in his suit and his hair is perfect and they're *on a date.*

Having a crush on August can be a bit intense, with the way he looks and moves and sings and laughs. James isn't likely to find a reason to be turned off since he already knows August extremely well after living together for a few years. He's familiar with August's habits and his quirks and the things that are likely to get on each other's nerves. He already knows he likes August as a person, so tonight is just to test if they're both interested in transforming that already established bond.

"What sort of prize?" August presses his knee further into James's and leans in while lowering his voice. "If we aren't going home yet, it can't be *that* fun."

James's face heats at the possibility, warmth flooding under his skin. It's not that he hasn't thought about it, but August insinuating something sexual between them has him hot and bothered and suddenly unable to focus on anything except how he definitely wants that. Maybe not tonight because who knows if they'll be ready, but it's an option. An option he's very excited about. When they left the flat, James thought he was the only one who was interested. By this point in the evening, it's very clear that August is shy but equally on board with the idea of giving it a go.

"I'll tell you if you guess right." James manages to answer, his eyes very purposely watching August's mouth for several seconds before heading further North where they belong. They are in a cab, after all.

"Hmmmm…either a secret underground concert, a pottery class so you can go all Patrick Swayze on me, or you've found an escape room and the two of us are about to have our first fight while looking for a hidden crocodile in a bookshelf." August seemingly had all of those ideas prepared, James laughing along as the possibilities reach new heights. They can always laugh together. Maybe that's why tonight is so easy. "What? You're competitive."

"Those are all excellent ideas, but no. Not even close." James chuckles once more then leans in as August had done, but closer, more intimate. He lets his nose brush against August's cheek as he mumbles, "But I'll keep those in mind for our next date."

This close, August is intoxicating, his smell overwhelming James's senses. When he pulls back, August visibly shivers, eyes fluttering while he watches James's every move. He looks like he's in a trance with James as his focal point. "So you…we're doing this again?"

"I wouldn't mind if we made a habit of it." James would love to spoil August like this every day, but they can't afford it. And even if he could, it'd lose its appeal after a while.

Tonight's very nice, but he wants to know what it's like to chill in their joggers and watch a match while snogging during advert breaks. James wants sleepy mornings in bed on their days off and holding hands as they walk through the park and sitting together at the dinner table for family events. "But not exactly this. Tonight was special."

Somehow, in the span of a month, James has gone from believing he was entirely straight, to accepting he fancied his flatmate, to seeing a future in a relationship with him, to being on their first date and on the way to making that future a reality.

"Yeah. I'll never forget tonight." August uses his free hand to mess with his hair, tousling the curls while James watches. He wants to ruin it with his fingers while kissing August for as long as he'll allow, but later. Maybe at home.

They have some fun to attend to.

"James! You *can't* be serious." August shoves at James, having disconnected their hands now they've arrived at their destination. "I'm in a suit!"

"You say that as if it's a bad thing." James steps out of the cab and offers his hand back to August. He doesn't need the help, but August keeps subtly asking for James to lead him through their date, and James is happy to oblige. "Besides, the suit can be removed."

"James!" August laughs loudly, letting his head fall back as his hand moves to his diaphragm, steadying himself. "I'm the worst golfer I know. Potentially the worst in London."

"A fact I'm well aware of." James lets August go first, walking into TopGolf together to continue their evening. This is one of the best ideas he's ever had. August just doesn't understand the brilliance of it yet. The worse August plays, the more *hands on* James can be. He's an excellent teacher.

They get up to their assigned platform with minimal hassle, James's reservation ready and waiting for them. It's a Monday night so they have the advantage of the place being relatively empty. There's a few other parties on their floor, what looks like a family down near the end and another date happening near the middle. James asks August what he wants to drink, orders a beer for the both of them, and shows him how to set up the game.

While James was away, August removed his suit jacket and rolled up his sleeves. Why does James find that so goddamn hot? Seeing August's forearms has James imagining things far too sexual for TopGolf. He slips out of his own suit jacket and sets it beside August's, but he keeps his arms hidden. If they both bare their skin, who knows what might happen?

"Why would we even bother keeping score?" August laughs, leaning his weight on his hand, hair falling forward into his eyes. James immediately wants to reach up and brush it away from his forehead. So he does, August following his movement then tucking his head down bashfully with a sweet smile.

"You might surprise me. End up being some sort of golf savant." James teases, waiting for August to glance up again because he's learning to love the way he's been looking at James all night. August is nervous, still, even as they've relaxed into their evening. And he's charming and hilarious and soft spoken, but there's something a bit like wonder in his eyes that ignites every time James reminds him that this is a date and not just spending time together.

"You're going first, otherwise you'll be laughing so hard we'll have to leave." August tilts his head toward the tee, waiting for James to get on with it already.

"If you insist. Let me just - " James reaches past August, getting entirely up in his space and holding him at the waist to steady himself. There were other ways to set down his drink but how else would he get close enough to press his lips to that point where August's perfect jaw comes to a perfect corner so close to the rest of his perfect face?

August holds his breath while James leans into him then lets it out in a surprised huff as James's lips graze his stubble. It's quite a feat considering the height difference, but James makes it seem easy, like something the two of them do all the time.

Before moving away, James lowers his voice to ask, "That alright?"

"Definitely." August mumbles, swallowing hard and holding James by the small of his back. James is glad to know he's not the only one ready to try being a bit more physical. Who knew flirting over golf could be such a turn on? "Don't know that I'll be focusing much on the game, though."

"I'm glad to be a distraction." James slides away from August and into his spot at the tee, making sure to really wriggle his bum and look a bit ridiculous to show that he's definitely not taking this seriously. August laughs at a particularly duck-like movement, covering his mouth to dull the sound when another group three spots down glares their way.

James takes a few easy swings to warm up, August whistling and cheering loudly when he hits one of the targets. He's ridiculous and James is unbelievably infatuated. "Hush, you."

"I'm in the presence of a professional." August gives James a sideways grin from his seat, legs crossed and beer in hand while he spins the glass distractedly. "It's quite a view."

"Put that confidence to use. Up with you. Come on." James waves him over, waiting for August to go through the process of rolling his eyes, heaving a dramatic sigh, and walking over very slowly to join him. "You hold this end."

James points to the handle of August's borrowed club, wondering if a dick joke would be too far.

"Good at handling poles, are you?" August elbows James out of the way and sets himself up (poorly) while James takes his vacated seat. Apparently dick jokes *are* on the menu.

"Wouldn't really know, sweetheart, but I'm hoping to find out." James cackles when August drops his club, cursing as he bends to pick it up again. "Something wrong?"

"Quiet, or I'll never hit the ball." August pushes his hair out of his eyes and sets his shoulders, focusing intently on the golf ball in front of him. For such a tall man, he's surprisingly intimidated by the tiny object.

James waits until August has already pulled his club back to say, "I'd rather you caress it, but to each their own."

August misses entirely, swinging hard until he's spun on the spot like a disjointed ballerina. The group nearby gives them another round of glares while James laughs loudly. He couldn't care less about a group of randoms. This is too much fun and August is wearing the frown of an annoyed puppy.

Adorably rumpled, August huffs and rests his hands on his hips. "You did that on purpose."

Instead of answering, James walks up to August and displaces his hands with his own in one smooth movement. He starts turning August, ignoring his very apparent gay panic at the contact, lining him up where he needs to be and arranging him in place. James slides a knee between August's legs, widening them considerably before bending him forward and reaching for his arms.

Swayze may have pottery, but James has golf and he knows what he's doing. "Course it was on purpose. Thought you could use some instruction."

"James, we are in *public*." August is as scarlet as James has ever seen him, clearing his throat and avoiding his eye, but allowing himself to be manhandled without hesitation. "And I'm officially not thinking about golf anymore."

"Shhhh." James had no idea he'd enjoy being so in charge of August like this, but it's making him imagine several other things they could be doing if they *weren't* in public. "Let's try a practice swing. Easy, just follow where I guide you."

August swallows hard then nods, letting James move his arms through a practice swing a few times while still plastered to his back.

"Relax, you're too tense." James's voice is low and soft, meant for August's ears only. It's barely a shade off from his bedroom voice, and it's definitely working its magic.

"You say that like I'm capable of coherent thought with you - when I'm - you're on top of me and I can't focus." August grumbles, making his point by shoving his bum back into James.

"Can't be having that. Back in position." James drops August's arms to focus back on his hips, setting him up again then stepping away. August literally whines but doesn't move, letting James retreat to safety before he swings again. "Now, just like I showed you. Easy back, easy through. Go on. Give it a go."

August hesitates, thinking hard based on the crease in his eyebrow. But then he lets out a sigh and executes an almost flawless swing. Once August realises he's actually done well he turns to James with a huge grin, eyes lit from within while he celebrates with his club in the air.

"I did it! I did - *Sorry* - " August drops the club suddenly when he realises the danger, James unable to stop the laugh that bubbles up through his chest as it clatters to the artificial grass. Sometimes he's a beautiful disaster, but he's so endearing. "I've never done that! It did the whoosh sound and went all the way out there!"

"That was well done." James confirms, laughing again as August encases him in a strong hug, arms wrapped around James like an affectionate cephalopod. It wasn't the most spectacular shot, but considering his skill, it *was* impressive. He's earned the hug. "Knew you had it in you."

"You're a good teacher." August breathes in deeply, surprising James with a hidden kiss to his temple as he steps away again and back to the tee, eager for another go. "I probably got lucky. Might need a few more lessons to make sure."

"That so?" James smirks, going back to his seat and watching August with a very pointed focus. How did he ever question his feelings when it's so completely obvious? The fondness and attraction he feels is constant whenever they're together. He just wasn't paying attention before. "Try a few more on your own. I believe in you."

August's next four attempts are complete misses, and James is starting to suspect he's not the only one playing a game. Now that he knows August is capable, he can recognise the excuse to have James's hands on him again.

"Just once more." James puts his arms around August and manoeuvres him like before, the two of them useless and giggly for an entire minute before managing to reel it back in. It's easily the best date James has ever had.

***

They spend the rest of their time at TopGolf laughing and flirting and finding any plausible reason to get their hands on each other. They're testing their boundaries in a new way, seeing what the other is comfortable with and what each of them is ready for. James is delighted to notice August steadily easing into his space, more touches in passing, more bumping into him, more glances that he doesn't look away from.

For two people who thought they were straight until *very* recently, they're having an excellent go of things. It helps that they're both in the same situation, both trying out a queer date for the first time, both exploring what it's like to exist in this way with someone they're already very well acquainted with.

"Hour's up already?" August asks as James glances at his watch and downs what's left of his beer.

"Don't worry, we aren't off home yet." James picks up August's suit coat rather than his own, holding it open to help August into it. "But we can walk to our next destination, and it's our last one for tonight."

"Escape room?" August slides his arms into his coat and turns back to James with genuine excitement.

"You keep bringing that up. Is this a hint that I need to be planning one for our next date?" James asks, shrugging into his own suit coat then giving his hair a tussle. He hasn't seen a mirror since he used the loo at the restaurant, but he hopes his hair is holding up alright. He'd tried to look as fit as possible, knowing tonight was his best chance to see if August might be interested, and so far it seems to be working.

"Could we? I've always wanted to do one!" August reaches for him, putting his hand on James's waist as he steps closer. "And you're competitive so you'd like it. We could even invite the others if you want? Maybe not Henri and Blair because of Junior and how he'd probably put everything in his mouth while he's teething, but Karim and Arthur would have fun. They're nerds."

"Double date?" James takes August's hand from his waist and interlocks their fingers. He really likes holding August's hand. It's so simple but it's quickly becoming a habit that he doesn't want to break. He likes how it feels to have August's hand in his own, to be aware of the calluses from his guitar and the warmth and breadth of his delicate fingers. It's thrillingly new but comforting at the same time.

"So where are we headed?" August doesn't drop James's hand as they walk back through the upstairs area and towards the exit. James knows it's risky, that even though it's the twenty-first century in a big city like London, they could be cursed out or worse. But if August's alright with the risk, he'll take it with him.

This is part of his life now, for better or worse. He's watched his friends deal with homophobia for years. James accepted it as a possibility, even a likelihood, when he began to understand his sexuality more fully.

"Somewhere familiar." Is the only hint James gives for where they're headed next. Dinner was romantic and golf was fun, but there's still one more important part of their evening. Something sentimental and soft and all those sensitive parts of himself that he's showing August more than ever.

They walk through the city for about fifteen minutes, but once they left TopGolf, August dropped James's hand. James looked to him with a raised eyebrow, mostly checking that he was still alright. August just glanced around and shrugged with a conflicted expression and James understood. Out here, where they're more exposed, it's more of a risk and August isn't comfortable with it. James gives him a smile and starts up a more in-depth conversation about escape rooms, letting August be excited and tell James why he's so determined to go. The more he talks, the more James looks forward to taking him someday soon.

When they're almost to their next destination, August stops them as they turn the corner, hand on James's elbow. He pulls James towards the brick wall of the building so other pedestrians can easily move around them.

"Why are you walking me to work?" August laughs, glancing down the road to where the cafe sits empty. It closed hours ago and won't reopen until his coworkers start their shifts before the sun, caffeinating the populace.

"It's a coincidence you work there. Not my fault." James reaches for August's hand only briefly, taking it in his own then dropping it again before tilting his head in the direction of the cafe until August gets the hint. "Go ahead. There's a reason we're here."

August rolls his eyes, but walks ahead of James, already taking out his keys to let them inside. He's allowed to come by after (or before) the cafe is open, within reason. The owner lets them all have access to use the space whenever it doesn't impact the business, and August and his coworkers have taken advantage for holiday get-togethers and birthday parties and sometimes a quiet study space, depending on their needs. They're all respectful and treat the place well, and there's never been an issue.

"Let's get inside and I'll explain." James comes up beside August as he unlocks the old door, shoving his shoulder against it to budge the lock into place. Hurrying off towards the back room, August rushes to shut off the alarm system while James closes and relocks the door behind himself and waits for August to rejoin him. He doesn't want to turn on the main lights and confuse anyone walking by, so instead he finds a lamp near where he plans to sit and awakens the space with its yellow light.

"Place is ours." August returns from the back with an apron on, James grinning and walking right up to him, tugging August in by his waist. He loves when August looks all domestic and sweet like this.

"You always look so adorable at work. Can't believe I didn't put the pieces together earlier." James sighs, hands running up and down August's sides while he stares at the absurdity of August in his nicest suit, a flour and espresso laden apron tossed on top with August's handwritten name tag on the left side of his chest.

"Sit. I'll make us something decaf." August gently removes James's hands, holding them as he steps away until the distance makes it impossible. Their fingers slide apart but they're both smiling. "And then you owe me an explanation."

"I won't forget." James's eyes follow August for a moment more, looking away when August catches him staring. His stomach swoops and he laughs to himself, turning away to take a seat at a very important spot, one that he hopes August will recognise as more than just part of his work environment.

James watches August behind the counter, letting himself process their night so far while August is busy. He thinks of their posh dinner and how it's easily the most romantic place he's ever taken a date. And golf was so ridiculous and fun, something he would do with friends, but it felt like an entirely new experience tonight. Dating someone he knows so well is what's making the difference more than dating a man for the first time. He's nervous because he already knows how he feels, not because it's someone new. The butterflies he gets are from August in his entirety, not some imagined version of a stranger he's just getting to know.

All of which makes their current location extremely relevant.

"Rooibos chai. Not too sweet, extra spicy. My favourite when I work the afternoon shift." August hands James a mug and takes the seat across from him, already bringing his own mug to his lips.

"Smells incredible. Thank you for making it. I didn't bring you here for this, but I appreciate it." James tries the drink, enchanted by the cinnamon, cardamom, and probably half a dozen other spices that warm his tongue. It's honestly a very kind gesture from August, something he didn't need to do but it makes this conversation significantly more cosy.

"So why did you then?" August crosses his legs, settling in to listen. Now that he's out of the apron, he's back to looking stunningly pretty in his suit. It's a bit distracting but James would probably feel the same about him in any attire.

"You realise where we are?" James puts his mug down on the coffee table between them, matching August's posture but setting his head on his hand, elbow propped on the arm of the chair.

"My work. Duh." August laughs, setting his mug near James's and sliding back out of his suit coat. James watches his muscles flex beneath his dress shirt, and then nearly chokes as August dangerously rolls up his sleeves again. Those damn forearms.

"Do you remember the first time we met?" James forces himself to stare into August's angelic face instead of gawking at his muscles. His daily exercise clearly pays off, even if he goes to the gym more for his mental health than for any form of aesthetic.

"Yeah, of course. We - *Oh.*" August's eyes go wide as his hands still, one of his sleeves only half rolled. "We met here. I answered your ad for a flatmate and we agreed to meet up after my shift."

"We sat in these exact chairs while we got to know each other and you made me some fancy latte I pretended to like even though it was too sweet because you were brand new at your job and then we stayed past close like we were catching up on a lifetime." James watches as August cycles through several emotions, his face moving and shifting while his eyes stay wide and bright. "We never technically agreed to live with each other that day, but we swapped numbers and I texted to ask when you could move in and the rest is history."

"I'd forgotten that. Or I guess I haven't really thought about it much since." August uncrosses his legs then crosses the other on top, rearranging himself before taking up his mug again. He seems nervous, but not uncomfortable. "Feels like a lifetime ago even though so much is the same."

"So much is different, too." James wants to fold himself into August's space, but not yet. He'll wait a bit longer and make sure it's what August wants. "I thought it'd be fitting to come here, where our story began, if we're considering starting something new together."

James pauses in case August plans to respond, but he's just staring, his eyes glassy while he remains unmoved in his chair. The same chair where James first laid eyes on him more than two years ago.

"I open at the close. The circle of life. The sunset before dawn. The beginning ends in the ending's beginning." James shrugs, quoting literary nonsense to try to convey his point. The writer in him will always search for words when he's reaching for meaning. "It could be the end of what we know, but the start of something different. Something entirely new for both of us. It's not a decision we should make lightly. You've already been in my life for years and you're integral. I don't want to lose you, but I also think we could be incredible as partners, if that's something you'd want."

"Oh." August says again, taking a deep shuddering breath and staring at James even more intensely than before. "Each happy ending's a brand new beginning."

"Exactly - wait, is that a song lyric?" James cracks a smile as August does the same, both of them breaking out into laughter just as they have consistently throughout their night. He's always wanted to be with someone he can laugh with, and August's laugh is like a melody.

"It's from *Enchanted*, that Disney movie where she goes to New York and sings to pigeons. There's a chipmunk involved." August settles back into his chair and takes another drink, still watching James thoughtfully. James has never felt like the centre of someone's focus this intensely. It's a bit of pressure he isn't sure what to do with, running a hand through his quiff as his stomach invents a new series of knots.

"We'll have to watch it sometime. You can sing along while I pretend to be annoyed just so I can listen to your voice. I love when you sing." James admits, not that it's really news to August, but it still feels like another crack in any semblance of keeping his cool. He sounds as whipped as Henri talking about Blair and the way they sing to Junior. James wonders if the stars in his eyes are nearly as bright, knowing they're likely approaching supernova based on August's pleased flush at the compliment.

"Can I ask you a question?" August sets his mug aside for the second time, further away as if he doesn't need it nearby for security anymore.

"I'm an open book, Augie. Tonight, I'm all yours." James hopes it's a question he has an answer to. There's a lot he still doesn't know about himself, or about the world and his place in it.

"Why did you ask me out?" August's mouth moves to the side while he considers for a moment before adding, "You asked me earlier why I accepted, but you didn't tell me why you asked."

"Told you I fancy you, didn't I?" James grins, deflecting the truer, deeper answer that's swirling between those knots forming in his mid region. "If not, consider this a confirmation. I fancy you and your pretty eyes and your swirly curly hair and your perfect smile and your warm hands. I could keep going, but I'll save the other reasons for later."

"I want the full list, but that's not really what I'm asking, as nice as it is to hear you say that." August is somewhere between pink and maroon but he looks happy, like he did earlier at the restaurant when James took his hand for the first time. "Why now? What changed for you?"

James takes a deep breath and lets his shoulders drop, trying to find the right words without making this about something it's not. The horoscope thing isn't the important bit, at least not right now. That's not what August needs to hear. "Henri came over and sort of gave me a talk. Got me to realise I fancy you. He was real gentle and nice about it, but once he pointed it out it was obvious. I spiralled for a few weeks but I managed. Not sure how you didn't notice because I could barely keep it to myself. I didn't accept it all at once because I'm far too stubborn for that, but he was right. I've been feeling this way for a while. Maybe the whole time."

"Was it that time he was over midday and asked us to visit?" August finally finishes rolling his one sleeve. James was distracted by it this entire time, but he's used to having to ignore those sorts of things that his brain tries to divert his attention to. "But that was weeks ago."

"There was something more recent, but I'm embarrassed to admit it. It was slightly selfish at the time." James stands up from his seat to pace around for a minute.

August watches him and lets him be, knowing that James needs to work himself up and out of a thought spiral sometimes and movement helps. James isn't truly spiralling at the moment, but his brain keeps going back to that night and how he felt and it's not a pleasant feeling.

"That night you brought someone home after your gig. When I stayed at Arthur and Karim's on the sofa." James turns to August, pausing his pacing until August nods his understanding, then taking it up again. "I thought I was going to be sick. Almost was, actually. I read your text and it felt like my world was ending and I knew I couldn't just ignore it anymore. Because you had every right to live your life and be with whoever you wanted, bring people home and enjoy yourself, but…I couldn't pretend I didn't want to be the person you took home anymore. Henri opened my eyes, but that night broke my heart open, and then I had *another* crisis and I called Arthur and we talked when I got to his flat and he told me about falling for Karim and how it changed his life and he gave me some advice and let me whine about having an unrequited crush on my straight flatmate."

"Well…" August interrupts James, accompanied by a soft smile. "Not that you knew it, and I wasn't sure either until recently, but your flatmate is fairly curvy."

"That's essentially what Arthur implied. Like he was mostly just there to be supportive and validate that I was definitely not straight and clearly had feelings for you, but he suggested I ask you out. I thought he was daft, but…" James finally stops pacing and falls back into the armchair across from August, still being watched like he's the centre of August's world.

"And you just woke up Thursday and thought you'd give it a go?" August is lightly teasing, still trying to get to tonight through James's spiral. It's continuous and sometimes suffocating from James's perspective, but August can usually follow. James sort of loves him for that and for his ability to ground him through it all.

"You, um, you sort of took a nap on me the night before? Maybe you don't remember." James decides it's too hot and takes off his suit coat to match August. Removing clothing isn't the point they're at, it's just too near stifling to keep it on. He's starting to sweat but it isn't from the heat of the room.

"I remember." August answers immediately. He looks embarrassed for the first time since they got to the cafe. "Since you called and asked me I've been doing a lot of thinking and…that wasn't an accident. Part of me wanted you before my brain caught up. I've always been drawn to you and thought about, like, your eyes and your smile and, um…I've even had a few dreams about nights like tonight. I sort of assumed everyone thought about their friends like that but I've learned that's not very heterosexual behaviour. I've wanted to cuddle up with you probably since the day we met, thought about it multiple times, and when I fell asleep on the sofa I was in the middle of this dream where we were napping together on a hill somewhere and the sun was in my eyes and I was laying on your chest and when I woke up you were there, just like my dream, and I just…followed what felt right in the moment. And the next morning I was panicking about it because I thought you would be mad or upset, especially when you called me out of the blue. Like when you asked about my break I expected a text about weekend plans or something, but the call had my anxiety at a level ten because I thought I like crossed a line or something. Some guys are fine with platonic spooning, but you're not very touchy feely."

"Oh shit, I hadn't even thought about that!" James leans forward, holding a hand out towards August as an apology. "I was so wrapped up in my own gay panic I didn't even think how you might be worried. Fuck, I'm sorry, August. You must've been anxious all morning and it's all my fault."

"It's alright. Turned out well, I think." August takes James's hand across the space between them. It's awkward and they both have to sit on the edge of their chairs, but August smiles at the point they meet in the same way as before. James wonders how many times they can hold hands before August gets used to it, how soon before they settle into being able to touch each other like this in a new context. "I'm glad you asked me."

"I'm glad you accepted." James grins, taking the chance to stand up, but he doesn't disconnect from August. He carefully manoeuvres around the coffee table until he's next to August's chair and he can squat beside him, their hands joined across August's knee. "And I hope it's not too presumptuous to say I think we've both been idiots who fancy each other and didn't have a clue."

"I'm not really sure what it means for me yet, but tonight's felt more important than any date I've ever had." August glances at James's lips before worrying at his own and sighing. "I get what you mean about not being able to ignore it anymore. Now that I know what's been going on with me, everything just makes a lot more sense. Being here with you, letting you take me to a nice restaurant and boss me around at golf and then walking me here, where we first met…"

"Sweetheart?" James asks, bringing his free hand up to caress August's face with a delicate touch. He brushes a curl across his forehead and behind his ear then tips his chin so they're staring at each other, cradled by the warm light.

"Yeah?" August wets his lips with the tip of his tongue, his eyes darting all around James's face while his breathing goes shallow. He's anxious rather than nervous, and James can't have that. He only wants this if August wants it too.

James uses his thumb to rub August's cheekbone and interlaces their fingers with his other hand. It takes a moment but August inhales a slow, steady breath and gives James a weak smile on the exhale. There he is. "Can I kiss you?"

August nods, already leaning forward and closing his eyes to meet him halfway. James slides his hand to cradle the back of August's head, bringing them gently together until finally, irreversibly, their lips meet in a hesitant kiss.

James keeps himself in August's space, letting him catch his breath without pulling away. August's hand leaves his and before James can wonder where it's gone, it's in his hair, pushing him forward until August's lips are on his own, so confident and sure that the wind is knocked out of James as he kisses back. August tastes sweet and his lips are warm and his hands are on James like he's a man starved and James is his last meal. It's a kiss with more passion than James has ever felt, his stomach doing an impressive amount of somersaults while they press into each other, learning their rhythm and exploring a new shared experience.

He can't kiss the way he wants from the squatted position he's chosen, so James pulls back as August's eyes go wide with concern, as if James is pulling away in rejection. But then James is on him, one leg between August's knees and the other on the outside of his thigh as he joins August in his armchair, a hand trailing through August's hair and the other sliding across the top of his broad back to pull his body close. Much better. They fit together well, James straddling August's thigh as their chests meet to deepen their kiss.

August holds James at the small of his back before sliding down the crest of his ass, making him gasp against August's lips as his hips rut forward in response. That's…new. James has never been *handled* like this before but he likes it. He really, really likes it.

"You're fucking incredible." James mumbles as he falls back into August's kiss, the devious smile he's wearing waiting to be erased. Now that they're comfortable, James slips his tongue past August's lips, relishing the deep noise of acceptance that August releases as James licks the roof of his mouth. He sends tingles through August's body that end in a shiver as he gets pulled down harder on August's thigh to give them both more friction.

"Best first kiss *ever.*" August groans, giving as good as he gets, and James is already hard in his pants. So much for wondering if snogging a lad would do it for him. It just had to be the right one: a man who smells like heaven, sings like an angel, and kisses like a very enchanting siren.

James loses track of reality while they move together, but by the time he thinks of removing all of their clothing to start enjoying the rest of each other, he remembers where they are and that August works here and they can't be having a filthy snog and potentially more in this armchair, as lovely as it is. Not enough space, to start with.

"August." James pulls himself away, his lips pleasantly warm and tingly while the rest of him is both relaxed and extremely turned on. This is what a good kiss is meant to feel like. He wants to kiss August for hours, trying out different rhythms and pressures and savouring each moment as it comes. "Not here."

"Oh shit." August laughs, hands moving from the back of James's thighs to his own face, running his palms down it like he needs a reset. "Sort of forgot. You're very distracting."

"So are you." James glances down where his semi is clearly pressing against the front of his trousers. August follows his gaze and makes a noise that James has never heard from him before, something mildly strangled and squeaky but ending with a muffled moan. Well then.

"We should, um…home." August meets James's eyes just as James leans in for another kiss. It's a *save it for later* quick press of their lips before he stands up and pauses their moment.

"You sure you know the way? I could google it." James teases while helping August back into his suit. If they keep removing and redonning these outfits, James might lose his mind. They're both wearing far too many layers and in too compromising of a space for what could be next.

"Pretty sure I remember, but you've been a good guide so far tonight. I think you'll get us there safely." August gives James a very meaningful smile, one that conveys how many interpretations he's intending for that statement.

"Still a date, even though we're heading home. Think we've earned another cab and I don't want to share you with the crowd on the tube." James slides an arm underneath August's jacket to hold him by the small of his back and press them together once more before they close up. August grins and leans down for another kiss, but James stops him after only a moment. If he doesn't, they may never leave. "We need to tidy up before we go. I'll help."

"It's alright, I've got it." August sighs because James is right. They can't leave their used mugs out even though he already washed up behind the bar.

"I insist." James takes both of their mugs before August gets the chance, but he waits for August to lead the way to the washing up area. When he mentioned the word partner to August earlier, he didn't only mean for romance or sex. If they're doing this, it's not going to be one of them taking care of the other, but a mutual give and take. August made the tea, James can help tidy.

Cleaning up together is actually just the thing, calming them back down from the heat they'd worked themself into and settling them into a more comfortable space to head home. This way there's no pressure for more from either of them, no expectation of what happens when they enter their flat together in this new way. They clean their mugs and make sure everything is right as they found it, then August closes up as usual to meet James on the pavement while they wait for their ride.

CHAPTER THREE

James helps August through their front door with a hand on his back, locking up behind them for the night. He's not quite ready for their date to end, but he would understand if August needs to be done, to have time and space to himself after all that's happened the past few hours. James consciously takes a steadying breath before turning around, knowing that August is still standing there waiting for him. Sure enough.

"Can I kiss you goodnight?" James slides his arms around August's middle and brings him close, August's forearms crossing on top of his shoulders while he stares down at him. There's several complexities held in his gaze but James doesn't have time to decipher them all before they're cleared away by a happy smile.

August leans forward and closes his eyes, James meeting him halfway. Much more calm than they'd been at the cafe, they kiss for a few easy moments before James pulls away, August lingering and trying to follow him for long enough that James knows he was a bit lost in it. Lost in James. And fuck, it feels really good to know he's not alone in this.

"Thank you for all of this." August takes a hesitant step back, one hand at his side and the other messing up his own hair while he stares hard at the ground. "The new plant and the fancy restaurant and flirty golf and then our quiet time at the cafe. It's been…revelatory."

"Would you be up for having a talk in the morning? You're working the afternoon shift, yeah?" James takes August's free hand and slips their fingers together once more before this night is over. He hopes it won't be the last time, but if it is, he'll cherish the memory.

"Did this go how you wanted?" August won't meet James's eye, suddenly shy now that they're truly alone. James gets the feeling that there's something he's holding back, but he's not going to push it.

"Oh, angel." James simpers, bringing August's knuckles up to brush his lips. "You exceed all my expectations. Just thought you might want some space to get your heart in order, think about things before we talk."

August nods, finally glancing up at James and leaning forward for one last goodnight kiss. Just a quick one. He walks away towards his bedroom, hand lingering just as his lips had until James has to let him go since he can't follow. He said he'd give August space and he meant it.

But when August gets to his bedroom he stands in front of the door, facing the dark wood without making any effort to actually open it. He's just standing there. Shoulders hunched, head bowed, looking a bit lost.

"August?" James asks gently, not moving any closer because he's pretty sure he knows what August needs, but it would be a hell of a miscalculation.

"Jay?" August still doesn't move, mumbling his answer, but it carries easily across the silent flat.

"Did you want to...?" James trails off, hoping August understands that he's both insinuating taking him to bed, but not wanting to force him to deny James outright. Something about having it be explicitly said seems unnecessary as he waits for August's decision. If it's a yes, he'll clarify.

It takes several drawn out breaths for him to reply, but August turns back around, hands fidgeting with themselves as he mutters, "Um...yeah, I think so...do you?"

James is moving before August even finishes his question. Walking confidently across the space between them, James pulls August in for a deeper kiss, pressing him up against his bedroom door and delighting in the response he gets. August moans as he melts,

96

kissing him back and letting his hands roam every inch of James he can reach. He's glad he guessed right.

"My room?" James barely separates their lips but August understands. He nods again, waiting for James to guide him across the living room and into his bed.

If James had any doubts a few hours ago, they've evaporated. August *wants* him. They still need to talk, but right now they both crave physical, sexual exploration together after several hours of holding themselves back with teasing and flirting and then drawn out, heated kissing. There's only one way to find out if they're sexually compatible. Technically there's several, but James isn't going to question this method when it involves August ending up in his bed.

"Please, James." August's hands frantically start to fuss at his suit jacket but they're shaking a bit and he's clearly desperate to be rid of it. James can't believe how many layers they're both still wearing. Ridiculous.

"Just to be clear, I'm taking you to bed for sex." James swats August's hands away and tugs him forward by his lapels, careful not to damage the fabric but hurrying them along in the direction of a horizontal surface. He wants August beneath him, to touch and kiss and worship. James has always been a very generous lover, but he has a feeling he's about to put his past experiences in a separate category. If someone was going to ruin him in the most exquisite way, he's glad it's August.

"And here I was hoping for a writing lesson." August, somehow, has found a spark of confidence to tease James even as they cross a threshold together (and not just the literal one to James's bedroom). August has an endless number of talents and James figures if there was ever a man to expose his latent homosexual tendencies…August is everything that excites him and so much more.

97

"Can I undress you?" James already has his hands beneath August's coat, ready to slip it off his shoulders and work on the rest of the many, many buttons in their way. Their next date should be joggers and *maybe* a henley. Nothing this complicated to remove.

"Can I return the favour when you're done?" August groans and lets his head fall to the side as James kisses along his jaw. He's noticed that it's one of August's weak spots, letting his lips drag, his tongue tease, his voice move through August's skin.

"If you're good, I'll consider it." James could be pressing his luck, but August seems to like the roles they've fallen into, kissing James again and letting himself be backed into the room. Taking charge, but still gentle, James guides August to the edge of the bed to sit, pressing a finger to August's lips to keep him quiet.

Forgetting any constraints of time and refusing to rush his way through this, James removes August's suit, carefully setting it aside on the armchair beside his wardrobe before moving on to his tie (quick work) and then his shirt. Each button undone is another kiss, August's hands resting against the mattress even as James untucks the loose fabric from August's trousers.

James takes a moment to admire him shirtless, hands brushing across August's chest and down his stomach, then back up to tangle in his hair. He's slightly in awe of how this feels, how completely right and equally thrilling to desire a man, to desire *August*, and to feel like he's becoming whole in the process. How the fuck did he ever think he was straight? "You're gorgeous, sweetheart."

August sighs, eyes sparkling as he stares up at James, staying quiet as requested. He's being *so good* and James is definitely going to reward him for it.

"Could I leave your pants for now, but remove your trousers?" James asks, knowing that even if August is up for this, he may still need some time to adjust. James certainly does, and he's had weeks longer than August to come around to the concept.

"Okay." August grins, leaning back further against his hands to give James easier access to his bottom half. He somehow seems calmer about all this than James, like giving himself the permission to ask for it was his last hurdle and now he's all in.

Maybe James should stop assuming and roll with August's ease. There will be plenty of time to talk later, tomorrow, this weekend, as long as August needs or wants. He should pay attention to what August is offering right now and worry less about the timeline.

Removing August's trousers is as simple as unhooking the closure and lowering the zipper, August groaning when James accidentally brushes the side of his hand against August's dick in the process. "Sorry."

"Don't be." August has his eyes closed tight, lifting his hips so James can get the taut fabric safely around his bum. Recently, as in the past few weeks, James has noticed how muscular and round and squeezable August's ass is, hoping to get his hands on it soon, and maybe even his mouth. He's had a dream or two about fucking August, but he forcibly reroutes his thinking because there's no way in hell that's happening tonight.

August's socks have to go, so James kneels before him, taking one foot in his hand and kissing along August's calf as he slowly rolls it down and off. He doesn't have any type of foot fetish, just a thing for August and the way he restrains himself the more James touches any amount of his skin. Maybe someday he can find out just how close to the edge he can take August with only his fingertips and a quiet afternoon in bed.

James borrows time to fold and stack August's clothes safely in the armchair already holding his jacket, taking care of every piece of tonight, every piece of August. It's a welcome responsibility. He's being watched, August furrowing his brow with a slightly gaping mouth, still splayed where James left him at the edge of the bed.

He's clearly not used to being looked after. James hopes to change that, to spoil him rotten and bury him in praise.

August finds his voice to ask, "My turn?"

"If you like." James undoes his jacket and tosses it on top of August's as he returns to the bedside, hand winding into August's hair for another kiss even as he stands up to do the same for James.

"I want to remember this." August mumbles, hands already loosening James's tie with a quiet confidence. He's being so open and vulnerable with James tonight, trusting him and allowing them both a chance at something entirely new together.

August clearly slows down now that he has James beneath his hands and ready to be derobed. It would be excruciating if it wasn't so sweet, the way August glows as he takes James apart. He said he wants to remember this, and James hopes it's not because he plans for it to only happen once. That might ruin him.

James cares about August so deeply as a friend, and now he knows what it could be like to be together. Truly together. He would live an altered life knowing they'd had this exactly once before August let him down gently. But that might just be James's anxiety because August seems intent on returning James's care in equal measure.

Once James is without a shirt, August runs his hands across James's skin, delicate and deliberate with an intense focus. James enjoys the breadth of the touch, the warmth and surety that transfers. August's hands are a song across his body as he whispers, "I like this."

It sounds like an admission, like he's not sure if he should be saying it. The hesitancy in words is a contrast to how he's acting, a sign of internal conflict that James can't puzzle apart.

"Hm?" James watches as August's fingers tangle through the curly strands on his chest. He trims as needed but prefers to leave his body hair generally as is and he's never had any complaints.

"Your chest hair. I like when you're scruffy." August moves a hand to James's cheek, caressing the stubble, keeping his fingers there as he gives him a sweet, slow kiss, his free hand moving behind James's back to hold him close like he's savouring the experience.

"Then you'll love me in the mornings after a long night of work." James attempts to joke, but August just grins and nods his agreement.

"I already do. Now that I know what's happening here - like how we both want each other or whatever - I understand why those days off were my favourite. I'd always think about snuggling up to you on the sofa because you looked so comfortable, but I'd let the thought just sort of pass me by. You're usually grumpy those mornings but...I like watching you be all forehead scrunchy and settled in the living room with your hair looking wild." August pauses for James's permission as his hands move lower, grasping the closure on his trousers but not making any move to undo anything yet.

"Go on then. I'm fine with being starkers, but if you'd rather my pants stay on that's fine." James gets a kiss pressed above his heart as August's hands slide beneath his waistband, pants and all, before meticulously undoing the closure. August is so careful with the zipper, watching his own hands and making sure not to touch James unexpectedly, even through the fabric. Not that James would mind, of course.

"Oh..." August pulls James's clothes halfway down his thighs and freezes, James's dick now free and hardening by the moment. August's hands have fallen back to his side as he stares, so James takes care of kicking off his own pants the rest of the way, leaning down to remove his socks while August watches with exceptionally wide eyes. He looks a bit stunned.

"Y'alright?" James asks, taking August's nearest hand in his own and bringing it to his chest to rest above his heart. After a few years of companionship, he knows that August needs to be grounded when he's anxious, and feeling James's steady breathing, the warmth of him against his fingers, that might help.

"It's just…" August blinks hard and meets James's concerned gaze, giving him a sideways smile. "I'm having a lot of extremely gay thoughts and feelings all at once."

"Too many?" James keeps their bodies separate, using his free hand to scratch at August's scalp reassuringly, the other still holding firm above his own heart with August's in the middle.

"No." August's eyes flutter a few times as James keeps up his caress, eventually sighing and dropping his shoulders. It takes a few more quiet seconds, but he opens his eyes again and slides into James for a kiss, pushing their bodies together and groaning the moment they connect. "So good."

James smiles against August's lips, bringing August's arms around his shoulders and holding him by the waist while they kiss. He doesn't normally enjoy snogging this much, but with August everything is so much *more*. "Is the bed too much pressure? We don't have to."

"I want to." August reaffirms his desire, leaning forward and waiting for James to take him where he wants to be. "Pretty much all I've been thinking about."

"Alright. Let's get you under the blankets." James walks August backwards a few steps, holding him at his side while he tosses the extra cushions to the floor and pulls back the sheets. Staying connected seems essential right now. "In you get."

"You're not joining me?" August asks, pouting. He's actually pouting. James rolls his eyes but internally he's melting. This is a side of August he's never really seen. They're playful with each other, and

August will sometimes whine until James brings him a blanket so he doesn't have to move from the corner of the sofa or something like that, but this open *need* for James, the submissive, hopeful side, is new. James completely adores him.

"Give me a minute. Keep your pants on." James tugs the sheets back up until August is fully covered, only his gorgeous honey brown eyes and tousled curls visible above the fabric. Hopefully he'll keep warm that way. "Just need to grab a few things."

"Oooooo, *things*." August mocks him, staying beneath the blankets where James stowed him. So good. So obedient. James has never had the chance to be with someone like this before, regardless of gender, but it's something he's always wanted.

He tries to hurry without looking like he's in a rush, gathering water from the kitchen and flannels from the linen cupboard then lube and condoms from where he'd stashed them in the loo a few days ago. Before he joins August under the sheets, James tells the Alexa to start one of his playlists through the speaker across the room. They're both musical people and it's nice to have a bit of ambience.

With everything they (probably) need within reach at his bedside, James brushes the curls from August's forehead as he lifts the sheets, waiting for August to scoot over so he can fit himself in beside him. It's a bit like arriving home.

"Fancy seeing you here." August grins, automatically folding himself under James. He's ridiculous, but James is already too far gone. It's nice that it can be easy like this, especially when the situation they're in is so new.

"Was thinking the same thing." James rolls on top of August, sliding a leg between his thighs and pressing their bodies together. He uses the kiss to recentre them both, get them back to where they were at the cafe when they had to bring everything to an abrupt pause. August's lips are sure and his hands are strong. James lets himself enjoy the moment for what it is. August is here in his bed, and it's the best reality he's ever known.

"Can feel you." August mutters, eyes still closed as he slides further down the pillow, taking James with him.

"I am vaguely smothering you in my bed." James teases, sparing a few kisses for August's neck and collar bones. August's skin is heaven beneath his lips, soft and warm and tempting.

"I meant..." August clears his throat, shifting his hips to convey his point, his own still covered dick knocking against James's for a moment.

"Well, sweetheart, you've got me all hot and bothered. But if it's - " James gets a hand quickly placed over his mouth as August giggles. James has never heard him laugh like that before.

"I'm not complaining." August drops his palm from James's lips and drapes his arms above his head on the pillow as he starts grinding their hips together instead, staring up at James with heated determination. James wasn't aware his hips were so talented. "Think I'd like to be naked now."

"Yeah?" James grins, hiding his face near August's shoulder to kiss that spot where his neck meets the rest of him. He's been thinking about it for weeks and now he finally has the chance. "I can help with that."

Moving lower beneath the sheets, James kisses along August's chest, his torso, across his stomach, while his fingers find their way beneath the waistband of August's pants. He watches August as his hands pull the fabric down and away, August's mouth open and eyes wide, like having James between his legs is a miracle.

The thing about August now being very naked and his dick being very close to James's face is that all he can really think about is getting August off and watching as he comes apart one gorgeous moan at a time. Can dicks be pretty? James's incredibly gay friends certainly think so, and August's definitely has an appeal... "Can I touch you?"

"Touch anything you want, fucking shit." August laughs, hiding his eyes behind his hand as a flush creeps up his chest. "You have no idea what you look like right now."

James smirks, sliding back up August's body but keeping his hands to himself for the moment. He kisses August, knocking his hand away from his eyes because he's too pretty to be shying away when there's nothing to be embarrassed about.

When August's body feels relaxed beneath him, his breathing even and deep, James tiptoes his fingers down August's chest, lips still sliding together, until he gets a grasp around August's dick and gives it one tentative pull, then another, and a few more until he finds a rhythm.

This isn't actually the first dick he's had in his hand, given his own anatomy and some past experience, so he has an idea of what he's doing. But August's is bigger, proportional to the rest of him, and holding someone else's dick is so distinctly different from holding his own.

Watching it happen in dark hallways at the pub or seeing it in porn holds nothing to the actual feeling, the awareness of what he knows through his hand, the opportunity for pleasure he can create. And in August of all people, someone so important to him, someone he wants to take care of, including but not limited to drawing exquisite orgasms out of him at every reasonable opportunity.

"James..." August whines, glancing down and breaking the kiss, then throwing his head back with his hands still above him and out of the way. James considers holding his wrists there, but he seems to be doing a decent job of it all on his own.

105

"Good?" James asks, cautiously continuing to move his hand, learning the veins, the ridges, the length of August. Sex has never felt so *intimate* somehow.

"I am *not* going to last long." August grumbles, waiting for James to kiss him again and keep his mouth occupied. But not yet.

"Open your eyes for me." James removes his hand and brings it up towards August's chin. He looks hazy, like he's already halfway to his release from just a few strokes. "Spit."

August skips a breath with another gasp of surprise as he brings his consciousness back enough to understand the command, glances down at James's waiting palm, then finally purses his lips and spits as requested.

"Good boy." James praises him, August groaning as his hips get involved again. God this is fun. "Hold your arms up and let me kiss you while I get you off and don't you dare be quiet about it."

"Yes, sir." August sounds remarkably breathless and fucked out. Where the fuck has August been hiding this submissive side and why did it take James so long to discover it? Hearing those words has James ready to growl. They're unbelievably compatible, and it's only their first night together.

Spit isn't lube, but James used the request less for friction management and more for an understanding of the dynamic. August was *made* for submission and James hopes they'll get to explore so much more of that together. A discussion for later.

For now, he plays with August's tongue, worries at his lips, drags his hand along August's eager dick, and marvels as they climb the hill to August's climax in tandem. August's hips move to the music that James would have already forgotten if August wasn't humming along every moment their lips lose touch, occasionally pressing a note into James's mouth like he needs to share it.

"James, I'm gonna - *soon* - so like - " August warns James between tongues and lips and the dance they manage even while the rest of their bodies are busy.

"Go on then." James moves his mouth to the side of August's neck, vaguely trying to find a spot to mark that won't get August in any sort of trouble. He decides on marking August's chest, that swell of his pec that shows through jumpers and brags about August's fit body beneath, hidden away from most of the world, but not from James. Not anymore.

"God, that feels good." August groans when James bites before sucking in earnest. Nothing too deep or harsh, but August seems to like it.

He likes it so well that before James is done with the bruise, August is shouting, his abs contracting as he starts to shoot spunk all down James's hand and his own stomach. It gets caught in the hair that leads to his dick, drips itself across the sweaty planes of his torso, falls down James's fingers as he keeps moving, listening to August and watching him in awe. That was the hottest thing he's ever seen, full stop.

"Christ, August." James removes his hand, reaching for a flannel to clean them both up as August pants and covers his eyes with one of his forearms. He's flushed red and one of his legs is holding James close as if there's anywhere else he'd dare to be. "I'm a changed man. Watching you let go like that..."

"You're...I'm...oh my god, James." August's free arm flails vaguely in James's direction, trying to find him somewhere in the abyss between them. Even though they're still connected by about 70% of their body mass, any separation feels like a canyon. August makes a sort of groaning whine that James tries to interpret, tossing the flannel off to the side to be tidied later.

"Shhhhhh." James noses up against August's ear, noticing he's even warmer than before. So many miniscule details he never wants to take for granted or forget for as long as he's given. Laying on top of August to cuddle and soothe him, James lets himself be held, August's arms coming around him as he presses a kiss to the top of James's head. He thinks it's meant to be some sort of thank you, August holding him close while his body recovers.

Even with the cleaning up, it's been less than a minute since August came, and James isn't rushing anything. His own hard dick won't need much prompting to release, even if he has to go take care of it himself in the other room. Working August into and through his orgasm is enough masturbation material for at least the next week.

"Sorry." August mumbles, kissing James's forehead this time. James has never had someone do that before. Not during sex. It's sweet, and it settles something in him that's been racing since August started to let himself go in James's eager hands.

"For what?" James tilts his face until he can meet August for a proper kiss, shifting his body around so he's less like August's weighted blanket and more like a cuddle partner.

"Made a mess." August blinks his eyes open to find James already staring. How could he not? August is a masterpiece, all lithe limbs and pink lips and tousled curls like some sort of Ganymede brought to life.

"Cleaned it up." James shrugs, kissing him again. To think an hour ago he'd never had the pleasure and now he never wants to stop. "And you never have to apologise for that."

"Okay." August sighs, dragging James to lay on top of him until they're fully aligned from tip to toe, or as close as they can get with their height difference. "Can't believe that was your first handjob. I swear you know tricks I've never felt before."

"Well…" James shifts to the side. August is in a talking mood and he wants to make both literal and metaphorical space for that. "I've had my own penis for a while."

He pauses when August laughs beneath him. The things he'd do to keep hearing that sound. "And that wasn't actually my first one."

"But I thought..." August runs a hand through his hair. Somehow it's still gorgeous, even all messy and sex rumpled. "Aren't I the first guy you've like...been with?"

"Definitely. That honour is all yours, sweetheart." James grins and takes over petting August's hair. It's becoming a habit to tangle his fingers in those curls. "But I dated a trans girl in uni for a month or so. Emma was great, but we didn't have much in common. She was super smart and into like computers and all that and I've always been more writing and books and occasionally sports. Didn't last long in a relationship but like...we did have sex. A lot of sex."

"Oh! That's - shit, I'm an asshole for assuming." August sits up a bit higher on the pillow with his back against the headboard, sliding out of James's grasp and causing him to sit up as well. "I don't know why I didn't think of that possibility. Now I feel icky."

"It's alright. To be fair, a lot of straight men won't date trans women. Which *is* transphobic, but you aren't." James sits across August's lap and plays with his hands. August won't meet his eye. "Until recently I identified as straight, right? Even though dating her didn't make me queer, being with you does. And like, she was actually really patient, knowing I had a lot to learn to make sex good for her and teaching me along the way. So for whatever skills I've maintained in that department, you'll have to send a fruit hamper to Emma."

"I'm sorry I assumed." August looks sheepishly up at him, genuine contrition written all over his face even though James isn't the one who's owed any sort of apology. "And like, just to be clear, I haven't done anything with anyone with a dick besides you, so I may need some coaching. Which...I actually don't mind at all."

"I'm well aware." James smirks, tracing August's cheek with his fingertips. His smile deserves a sonnet. "What do you think TopGolf was for?"

"I assumed you wanted to shake your ass and show off." August shrugs, leaning into James's hand with his cheek. "Turns out I like when you're in charge."

"I like taking care of you. Glad it's worked out so naturally." James presses into August for a relaxed snog, August's hands finding his thighs and exploring a bit. It's just so easy like this, chatting between orgasms and sharing themselves, body and soul. James could do this for hours. Maybe for a lifetime.

"James, I - I want you." August pulls back from James to glance down between them. James's dick is still half hard and pressing against August as they kiss and it seems to be pulling his focus.

"You have me, angel." James taps under August's chin to get his attention. "I'm not going anywhere."

"I know, but I meant, like - " August takes a deep breath, like he's trying to decide how much to say, or how to say it, fitting the words into the right shape before he shares them. "I want your dick. Up here."

He tilts his chin up and away from James's fingertips, indicating he wants James to straddle his face, or so it seems.

"Want me to wear a condom?" James asks, already reaching for one where he set it on the table beside them.

"No, it's alright. I know you get tested, but, um," August tugs at James until he's sitting across his lap again. "We should probably both get checked again before we consider like going without one for anal. *If you want - we obviously don't have to do that if you don't want to.*"

"No need to panic, I definitely want that eventually." James readjusts so he can kneel up when it's time to get his dick near August's face, if that's still what he's interested in. "I agree about us both being safe. I use protection with everyone, and there's plenty of times I've worn one for a blowie. Don't have any flavoured options on hand, though. Sorry about that."

"I'm fine going without for this if you are?" August scratches nervously at the back of his head. "Like I know the risks, but neither of us has any symptoms as far as I can tell, and we're both good about getting checked. But I kind of just want your dick in my mouth, and I'm not worried about it. Like if you were a stranger it might be different but, honestly? I know where both of our dicks have been."

"Oh?" James starts to move himself on top of August with a smirk. He may not have August's rhythm, but he knows what he's doing. "Been keeping track, have you?"

"Maybe." August flushes, pulling James in closer until they're kissing again. It's clearly a distraction so James doesn't ask any follow up questions, and it's very effective. He knows that come tomorrow morning he's definitely going to be asking August just how long he's been keeping track of James's casual sex life and if that maybe shouldn't have been a hint that he was feeling a bit more than friendship for a while.

"I'm fine with it, to answer your question." James presses his words into August's lips, savouring the smile he gets in return. "But we'll have to chat more before we do anything else."

"Deal." August slides his hands under James's thighs and pulls up until he's kneeling, James laughing but letting himself be handled. August is very strong and James likes knowing it through shared intimacy, his muscles serving a very specific purpose.

"Scoot down." James brushes his fingertips through August's hair just because he can and waits for him to shift further down in the bed. "Comfortable?"

111

He nods, so James takes himself in hand and works his fingers over his dick a few times, staring deep into August's bright eyes. "Open up."

And like the obedient man that he is, August does, eyes still locked with James and hands warm at his waist.

Knowing it's August's first time, James starts with just the tip of his dick against August's lips, tracing them for a moment before letting the first few inches inside his mouth. August's lips immediately close around him, pulling him further inside with a gentle press to his back with his broad hands. James is careful because August's never done this before, so he lets himself be moved, but only just, keeping half of his dick still exposed to let August adjust to the feeling. He moves himself forward and back again, small withheld movements, just to let August know what it'll feel like. James is so focused on keeping August comfortable that he's barely registering how it feels for himself yet.

"Stop me if you need to, alright?" James pulls himself off until his dick falls from August's mouth so he can respond properly. They should've talked about that before. He'll make sure next time.

"Maybe we should…like is it easier if you lay down and I'm on top of you?" August trails one of his hands to James's dick and starts moving it along the shaft, easy as anything, like he's done it a dozen times before.

As an answer, James drops himself from August's grasp and flops back against one of his pillows, hands already reaching out to bring August with him. "Definitely easier, if you still want to. You don't have to, you know."

"I know." August gives James another kiss now that they're horizontal again, but he's sweet about it, a twinkle in his eye and a sideways smile when he pulls away. "I really want to. Just that preview had me wanting so much more."

"Come here." James grins. He knows he looks love sick and drunk on August and he couldn't give a single fuck. And he's not the only one, August equally as enthralled with James.

They snog for an amount of time that could be an hour but is likely several delicious minutes before August starts moving down James's body, stopping to hover once his head is between James's thighs, holding himself up in an extraordinarily sexy push up. James swears his dick gets harder as he takes in the bulge of August's biceps and considers how much he could hold.

It seems August is done talking for now, because he wordlessly shifts himself into position, left arm supporting his weight as his right hand moves to James's dick. He waits for their eyes to meet one last time before falling into it, taking James in his mouth and using his hand to make up the difference like he's had practice. James groans, already tempted to start thrusting into August's mouth and having to make a concerted effort to hold back. God, August's mouth feels *so good*.

"What do you like?" August pulls his lips away but keeps working James with his hand, his spit dribbling a bit along James's dick where he's already started to make a mess. "I read up, but each dick has a preference."

Was that a joke? He's sucking James's cock and making a joke? James is so fucked in so many ways.

"I, um - fuck, August." James lets his head drop back against the pillow to gather his thoughts for a moment, but now August's fingers have moved to his balls and it's very hard to focus. "That. I like that. And a lot of pressure from your lips right at the tip. Match your hand to your mouth if you can, but honestly this is already amazing."

August nods and gets back to it, doing exactly as James asked with very little adjustment. All James can think about is his tongue and his lips and *god* the suction he's managing. James has had many blowjobs in his life, and while they all share similarities, so much is different with August. His hand covers so much more than he's used to, his mouth is bigger, his stubble occasionally meets the inside of James's thigh, and the knowledge that it's August, someone who knows him and might even love him, that he's the one putting himself in such a vulnerable position to pleasure James…it's almost too much. Also where did he learn how? Even if he read up as he said, he's translating that knowledge into action incredibly thoroughly.

"August, I'm close." James pants, wondering when his hand wound its way into August's curls yet again. He's not pressing August in to choke and gag, just holding him, grounding himself in a way. August has that effect on him.

Instead of pulling away, August hums, the vibration felt through James's dick, and keeps going. With a confidence to be admired, he uses his left hand to reach around and pull James's cheeks apart, tracing delicately from his ass to his balls like a feather along his perineum. James shivers and wonders again where the fuck he learned to do that.

But almost without warning, his orgasm hits him. It's only after he's shouting August's name that he realises it's because August had been holding him off with a firm grasp near the base which he let go in time to push his mouth the furthest down he's dared yet, James's dick just tapping at the back of his throat. August chokes a bit, James's cum spluttering out of his mouth as his right hand keeps steady through it, wiping away the mess he's made of his face with his left.

"Up here." James scrambles for August's shoulders, pulling him up and into a heated kiss. Fuck the mess, he just wants him as close as he can get, tongues hot and wet as they slide together. James rubs himself against August until he's really done, breathing heavy and body overheating with no intention of pushing August away anytime soon.

But despite the extremely satisfied warmth he's feeling, they do need to be cleaned up a bit. James meanders his hand around the table until he finds a clean flannel where he left it. He starts with August's gorgeous face (carefully of course) and then wipes at his own stomach and general cock area until it seems sufficiently cleaned for the moment.

"Stay here with me?" James asks, tossing the flannel to join the rest of the mess on the floor and hoping with his entire heart that August spends the night. Tomorrow, maybe a morning shower together, fall back into bed for a quick shag, a lazy afternoon nap, and then the rest of their lives. Something like that.

"Sleepover?" August nuzzles his face against James's jawline, pressing a kiss behind his ear before getting settled against James's chest. "Your room has its charms."

"Not tired yet, just want to be together." James admits. They both need to decide what it is they want from this, but at least for tonight, he wants August in his arms and sharing his bed, cuddled up and happy. "But if you - since we're done, if you'd prefer space - but I'd rather you stay, if that's alright."

"Hmmmm." August pretends to think it over, kissing noisily all over James's face until he's pushed away with a laugh. He could get used to being adored by his own personal giant angel. "You are very cuddly. All warm and soft and you."

"Just want to lay here and talk a while." James buries his face in August's hair as he resettles across James's chest like a very overgrown koala. "You're sort of my favourite person."

"Mmmmmm." August hums in agreement, kissing James's chest with his eyes closed. If he dozes off, James won't be surprised. It's been a long night. "I'm so happy."

James feels something alarmingly like tears behind his eyes, so he keeps one hand in August's hair and uses the other to draw lazy circles along his back, holding him close. A month ago he had no clue he ever wanted this. Now he wonders how he went so long without it.

***

It's beautifully quiet and still while James stares up at his ceiling with August's head resting on his stomach. James is reclined, not quite upright, August diagonal across his lap so he can fit on the bed. He's so tall, his toned limbs lazily draped in James's direction while they cool down and relax. Maybe they should consider pushing their beds together like in one of those student halls. Probably best if they splurge on a new bed together.

But James is getting ahead of himself. Way too far ahead of himself. He doesn't want to hope for too much and end up destroyed when it doesn't happen.

They finished having sex a while ago and now they've settled into each other, neither of them wanting to move away or go to sleep just yet. But August committed to stay the night, and James swoons every time August reminds him (four times in the last hour, but it's not as if he's counting). This is the most at peace James has ever felt, his mind quiet, his body sated, his heart at rest.

"Like when you play with my hair." August mumbles, eyes closed as James's fingers tousle his curls. He didn't even realise he'd been caressing August yet again, a floaty sort of feeling holding him in place, like the romantic overture playing through the final kiss of some old black and white film.

And then even quieter, he adds, "I like you."

"Yeah?" James grins, his gaze going soft as he appreciates August casually existing in his space. He's not usually much of a cuddler, but with August he's drawn to it. He wants the softer moments just as much as the heated or silly or serious ones. Maybe it's realising he's queer or specifically his feelings for August, but he wants things he's never really considered before. Long term, sappy, emotionally significant things. "I like you too, sweetheart."

"Promise?" August's eyes are still shut but his face subtly changes, holding more tension than a moment ago. Like he's worried this was all some sort of joke, or that James isn't completely ass over elbows for him.

"Look at me?" James asks gently, one hand still carding through August's curls, not moving from the comfortable shape they've found themselves in. "Maybe we should chat now instead of in the morning? But if you're too tired or want more time to think that's fine."

"No, I'm awake." August gives him a sleepy smile and yawns despite his easy reassurance. He's so fucking cute that James has to hold back a sigh. His heart eyes must be visible through time and space, like the Northern lights or a full moon on a clear spring night back home in Bray. August makes him so damn poetic it's embarrassing.

"What are you thinking about? You seem contemplative." James slides his hand from August's curls to his chest, rubbing soothing circles against his skin like it's second nature to comfort him with his touch. Maybe soon it could be.

"I think I'm gay." August answers after a pause. His voice is soft and steady while he comes out to James, glancing up to meet his tender gaze with a twitch of a smile. "Pretty sure, actually."

"Like *gay* gay or…?" James trails off, sitting up straighter but keeping August in his lap. He likes being able to cradle him like this while they talk. James has always been a bit protective of August, more so now that they're whatever they are. He'll get to that in a minute.

"Like fruity homosexual boy fucking dick riding cock worshipping gay." August giggles, his smile growing and tilting sideways. "Tonight has really clarified some things for me."

117

"You're welcome?" James laughs as well, his torso bouncing with the sound as August continues to grin up at him. These tender moments of conversation are certainly different than how things were between them before. James likes it. More than likes it. He wants this with August as often as he can have it.

"Remember how depressed I was after ending things with Martha?" August asks, taking the hand that James has been trailing along his chest to hold in his own, intertwining their fingers and watching how they fit together. Watching the puzzle of their bodies form a picture seems to settle something in August, a calm overtaking his features.

James nods when August looks to him for some sort of confirmation. But August needs to talk and James will always listen, so he keeps quiet and waits for August to sigh before continuing. It seems like this may have been weighing him down for a while.

"I thought something must be wrong with me. Like, I'd get in these relationships or go on dates and it was…fine. Nice, even. But it was never what I thought it would be. I didn't burn for them, you know? I don't want to like discredit those experiences or say I didn't like them, because I did, but now that I know the alternative, I think I was just sort of going through the motions. Wondered if I might be asexual but that label didn't feel right either. And like I could have sex with them and it was good but it wasn't half as good as just kissing you at the cafe. You touch me with a pinky finger and my skin comes alive. You graze your lips on my cheek and I forget to breathe. You hold me and it's like my universe has a gravitational centre for the first time." August laughs at himself, at how infatuated he's admitting to being.

When James kisses their joined hands, August swallows down some unnamed emotion before finishing his thought. "I'm sorry, I know I'm not making much sense. It's just…this is what it's supposed to feel like. I've wondered about my sexuality before, figured it would be obvious if I was gay since I've known queer people my whole life and it wasn't like I was avoiding it or anything. But after Martha…I really tried to love her like that but it always felt hollow. I knew something wasn't right beyond our specific relationship issues. Even talked with Blair about it a while back, that day we went to the gardens. They let me talk myself in circles, but I could tell they had a lot of thoughts they weren't sharing, and now I know they recognised a lot of what I was going through…And then I had that night after my gig, when you went to Arthur and Karim's place, and it was *fine* but it still wasn't quite right. We got off and whatever but I didn't *feel* anything…now I know why."

"That sounds a bit overwhelming. Even though it's nice to figure out who you are and have a name for it, it's still an emotional undertaking." James has never truly appreciated August's mind before. Not like this. They've never had this deep of a discussion of the intimate matters of self and soul.

"It *is* overwhelming." August looks up at James again, the side of his face grazing across James's lower abdomen in the process. It's not inherently sexual to be this close, but it's endearingly intimate. There's no shame between them in their naked, sex-used state. "But I'm also so happy, Jay. Like I can't explain it properly but I feel like I have clarity, like something that's been gnawing at the back of my mind for a really long time is finally gone. You took a chance and asked me out and it probably changed my life."

"You've changed mine, too. I thought I was straight until you showed up." James pokes at August's side just to watch him happily squirm then resettle with a huff. "I don't think I'm gay like you, probably pan or bi or something. I'll figure it out later."

"So no big revelations for you tonight then?" August glances unceremoniously at James's naked dick just inches away from his face, like he's remembering the things that dick and the person operating it have already taught him tonight. "No yearning for a life you've been missing?"

"There's that as well, just in a different way." James feels nervous for the first time in hours. But he's already taken the lead tonight in so many ways, so what's one more? "Been thinking about how nice this is. You and me, like this. Could get used to it…"

"Is that what you want?" August sits up, James already missing his warm weight across his body. But then he rests beside James with a hand on his knee, waiting for an answer as a silken curl falls over his eyes, and James is so supremely fucked, but maybe in a good way.

"I don't want to rush you into anything. You've only known you were gay for a few hours and it's fine if you want to like…live that life for a while." James winces but he hopes it's not too visible.

He does want August to do what's best for himself, even if it might hurt him more than a little to watch it happen. And maybe that's the best proof he could have that this is very real, that wanting what's best for August, even if it means he takes a step back, shows a respect and a love for him that's clearly deeper than any romantic or sexual relationship he's had in the past.

"If this is your time to go to the gay clubs and try out poppers and back room hookups and experience your identity to the limits, I don't want to stand in your way. I know how much it meant to my mates to have those experiences. Helped them find their way and be free and open in a new way. I wouldn't judge you if you did, too. Not as if I didn't do plenty of that myself back in the day, just in a more heterosexual direction at the time."

"Could you look at me for like three seconds instead of staring off dramatically into the distance and pretending you'd actually be fine with that?" August places his right hand on James's cheek and waits, bringing his leg over so he's straddling James's lap while sitting back on his heels.

James hadn't even realised he was avoiding August's gaze. He didn't think he could watch his heart get broken in the reflection of August's eyes so he'd momentarily shut himself away. But there's a warm palm on his face and strong legs bracketing his thighs and he'll manage. "Meant it, though. If that's what you need, I'll respect it.

You're still young and you deserve the fullness of your life, whatever that means for you."

"I'd rather be with you, having lazy afternoon sex and kissing in the constant London rain and arguing about sports and flirting via text and cuddling while we sleep between our ridiculous schedules. I know it's quick, but it's also a long time coming. I know you, babe. I know that I want you." August leans in to leave a warm kiss on James's lips, both a promise and a hope.

James brings his hands up to hold August by his lower back as he falls into it, letting August's decision flow through him like that first sip of strong tea the morning after a very long night, reawakening his senses slowly but steadily.

With James still holding him like glass, August continues. "I don't need Grindr and clubbing and all that. Not really my speed. But oddly enough, the only time I've enjoyed that scene is with you at my side. I'm not in your bed tonight because I've just realised I'm gay and you're willing and a total smokeshow. I'm here because I want you, specifically. You, James Joyce Dolan, with your sparkling eyes and your lilting accent and your grumpy mornings and just…all of it. I want to be your boyfriend, if you'll have me. Decided that when you handed me my new plant before we left for dinner."

"Of course I'll have you." James rests their foreheads together, smirking when he feels August playing with his hair. Maybe it's a mutual habit. That little speech was everything he needed to hear, delivered with August's signature warmth and earnest emotion. "I want all of those things you said and so much more. You're the first person I've really wanted any of that with, which might be why it scares me a little. You already matter so much to me and this is just the very beginning, if we're lucky."

"That's settled then." August shifts his hips until they're in a more sexual position, starting to move slowly on top of James like he's ready for another round of orgasms. It's a drastic mood shift, but it's also a continuation and an indication that he meant what he said. He wants James, specifically, and not just because it's convenient. Good thing they're still naked because James *loves* moments like this, August showing his confidence in a way James can literally feel. "Besides, if one of us wants to go out and get laid, I don't see why we couldn't just do that together."

"August..." James groans, moving his hands to August's hips to hold them in place because he's about to get off ridiculously fast if they follow that trajectory. Not yet. "You'd want that? Like being open but together?"

"Definitely." August holds James's face in both of his hands, like James is the most important thing in the world. And like the good boy he is, he doesn't fight James's hold, stopping his dick grinding until he's given permission to continue. "We'll have to set boundaries, obviously, but I have so many kinks I've never explored and a lot of them involve more than two people."

"You're going to be the end of me." James kisses August again, rolling them over in the bed so they're laying down with James on top. Seems it's time for round two.

"Also I'm a Leo and we're like fiercely loyal. Even if we fuck other people, at the end of the day I'm still yours." August says like it's nothing, like it's a given that he wants to be James's boyfriend but also have interesting, non monogamous, kinky sex together, as if they've discussed it a dozen times before. James's world is about to get so much more interesting. "There's a lot of reasons I'm *such* a Leo. We're incredible at sex."

"So I've noticed." James stops talking so he can kiss August for several heated minutes, tugging on his hair and grinding against him and falling even further for his *boyfriend* because that's a thing now. He's never had a boyfriend before but there's a first time for everything.

But there's something bothering him after August's comment about being a Leo, an intrusive little voice in the back of his mind that won't shut up until he pulls back and straddles August, almost perfectly mirroring how they'd been sitting just a few minutes ago. "Wait - "

"What's wrong?" August is breathing heavily, flushed and half hard beneath James with very concerned eyes. He searches James's face then looks between their bodies. "Did I - "

"No! It's nothing like that. I just need to come clean about something." James laughs at the absurdity of it all. Who would've thought his silly side job would end them here. "Was going to tell you tomorrow if things went well, but - "

Climbing unceremoniously off of August, James gets out of the bed for the first time in over an hour, searching the pockets of his discarded clothes until he finds his phone. He probably shouldn't have left it buried in a pile of fabric on the floor, but he had other priorities.

"You're scaring me." August sits up against James's headboard and tugs the sheets to cover his lower half. "Should I be worried?"

"No! Sorry, I'm making this dramatic. It's stupid, really." James sits beneath the covers with August, close enough that their thighs rest together as he hands over his phone, already open to the twitter account for the magazine's horoscopes. "Remember how you told me about that opening with the magazine? How you said it would be easy money for me?"

"You didn't." August grins like he's won the lottery, snatching James's phone away from him and immediately starting to scroll. After a moment he shakes his head and types *Leo* into the search function and resumes scrolling, various emotions flickering across his face. "How long have you been doing this?"

"Um…a few months? Basically since right after you mentioned it. It's just the daily tweets and then the weekly long form horoscopes for the website." James slides his arm between August's waist and the pillow, setting his head on August's shoulder to cuddle. God, he's such a sap. "It's actually why Henri confronted me about this whole situation. He'd gotten it out of me from the beginning that I was writing these and that I was using all my mates as inspiration, right? And once he realised you're a Leo..."

August drops the phone and surprises James by tackling him back against the pillows. James is really liking their dynamic, how August can throw him around like this just as easily as let himself be thrown around, tossing each other gently into love with a healthy dose of fun.

"I've been an idiot, telling Tiff and everyone else how good the horoscopes are because they *always* apply to me. I should've figured it out months ago! I'm literally the one who told you about the job, but I had no idea you took it." August kisses James hard three times in a row before removing himself and going back to the phone so quickly that James has whiplash, left desperate and staring while flat on his back beside August's naked hip.

"Didn't know how you'd feel about it, so I didn't tell anyone but Hen. Impossible to keep anything from him." James pushes himself up onto his side and starts drawing patterns on August's thigh, daring to creep his fingers steadily closer to August's dick.

"Oh my god, babe! This is embarrassing!" August laughs, setting the phone on James's bedside table and climbing on top of him yet again. "How did it take you so long to realise you're into me? You're *so* in love with me. You've got it bad, talking about my laugh and my eyes and all that."

"Yes, well, you have many admirable qualities." James protests, flushing at August's teasing. Maybe he should've waited to tell him til tomorrow like he planned. "We're together now. It's allowed."

"Damn fucking right we are." August looks at James with an intensity he's never quite seen before. If eyes could blaze, August's would rival the sun. "Tomorrow morning, before breakfast, I want you to fuck me until I forget my name. And then tomorrow afternoon I want

124

to ride you until you're so deep I can feel it for the next week. Never been fucked before, but I have a feeling I'll be a slut for it. Been curious for *months* and I had a dream the other night. A very specific dream..."

James moans way too loud, and he'd be concerned about that, except he has other priorities right now. Mostly tumbling around with his boyfriend in his bed for a while longer before they go to sleep. "What time do you work tomorrow? Trying to plan around it, be respectful of that gorgeous ass and the schedule it needs to keep."

"Not working tomorrow. Called off while you went to the bathroom at the restaurant. I had a feeling." August throws his arms above his head in supplication when James puts just the slightest pressure in that direction. He's so obedient and willing to go where James guides him.

"But you don't want me to fuck you tonight?" James clarifies, moving down August's body and getting ready to return that blowjob from earlier. His mouth is starting to water just thinking about it and this increasing confidence from August is sexy as fuck. "I'm literally at your disposal."

"Nope." August's breath catches as James licks the tip of his dick and then lets it into his lips, barely applying pressure, one hand holding his hips down to remind him to keep still. "Was hoping you'd finger me until I see stars and blow me while you do it. Never had anyone find my prostate before, but it sounds fun. When it's my turn I want to rim you before blowing you again. Really enjoyed that earlier and I spent most of our time at TopGolf staring at your ass and wondering what it'd taste like."

James lets August's dick drop out of his mouth with a surprised chuckle. He plans to do exactly as August asks, look after him and make him feel every beautiful sensation he's capable of. "And then it's bedtime. We've had a long day."

August manages to roll his eyes but he nods, squirming beneath James's hands impatiently. "What are the chances you want to tie my wrists to your headboard?"

"Christ, August. How many different shades of grey do you contain?" James pushes himself back up to get off the bed, already in search of his least favourite tie since he's positive it's about to be ruined.

"Fuck grey. I'm the entire rainbow." August laughs at his own joke, pushing the sheets all the way to the foot of James's bed and laying himself out like a gift that James has unwrapped. Has August read some sort of 'How to be a submissive partner' guide? He's a living wet dream, and James's dick is heavy between his legs.

"That you are sweetheart." James snatches the satin tie from his wardrobe and hurries back to the bed with it, August already lifting his wrists in anticipation. He gets up near August's face, nosing along his jaw and lowering his voice. "Want you to cum in my mouth. Think you could do that for me? Behave and let me take care of you?"

"I'll be so good." August's eyes are already slightly glazed over as the fabric slides across his wrists. James doesn't bother to tie the knot very well, leaving more than a generous amount of space since it's mostly for aesthetics. Pressing a kiss to August's open lips, James readjusts his loose limbs to be in a more comfortable position before getting himself back between August's legs.

James gets August to take a few gulps of water then finishes the glass himself before picking up the lube from his bedside table. He dribbles a healthy amount on his fingers, spreading it around to get it warm before applying it to August's ass. If August's never had anything inside of him before, James is going to take it so slow he'll be literally begging for more.

He wants August's first experience to be as safe and comfortable as he can make it. "Once you adjust, I want you to ride my fingers while I choke on your cock. Learn what you like, find what feels good, and tell me to stop if anything hurts or if you need a break. Consider it an order."

August makes a simpering noise, halfway between a moan and a whine before squeaking, "Yes, sir."

And there's that title again. August has a long list of kinks, and apparently one of them involves being a perfect, pretty submissive. James hasn't given a blowjob in years, but he remembers the general idea. He needs one hand on August's dick to accommodate its size while the other is busy spreading lube around August's rim, his mouth already moving back to take August in again. Giving can be a full body experience and James is definitely ready.

But before his mouth is busy, James adds, "Ride my fingers like you want to ride my dick tomorrow. Give me a preview, sweetheart."

And August does exactly as requested. He moans and yells and shouts James's name as he releases down his throat, waves of pleasure that he's never experienced before flowing through his body while James continues to work him through it before cleaning them up. When James unties his wrists, kissing each one delicately and pulling August to lay on his chest, August snuggles in close while he catches his breath.

"Love you." August mumbles, kissing the side of his neck while being brought back down to earth by James's patient, delicate hands. It's certainly not the first time he's said it, but it does have an added layer now. "Figured you should know."

Huffing out another laugh in surprise, James kisses those sweaty curls he adores. Maybe someday he'll stop being surprised by the way August can go from filthy fucking to sweet conversation. "Love you too, Augie."

When the tender moment has begun to taper off, James shares a thought he's been holding inside for several minutes. "You know, I think I like giving head. Could get used to sucking you off and hearing you shout my name. Very powerful feeling, that."

August smacks James on the chest, but it's so light it barely registers. He's still orgasm hazy, his muscles heavy in the best way. "I was being sweet."

"So was I. And so was your dick." James teases, loudly smacking his lips to prove a point. But he actually did sort of enjoy the taste. Not on its own, but the knowledge of what it is and where it came from and how it got in his mouth. Plus August tends to eat fairly healthy, which, according to his friends with more experience, makes a difference in how spunk tastes. "Not sure why anyone would want to spit that out. Like liquid gold."

August groans his annoyance and James lets himself be manoeuvred into a new position now that August is recovered. "Lay down and let me ravish you, Jay."

"Gladly." James pulls August into a kiss first, the contrast of taste between the spunk still coating his mouth and August's tongue a heady combination. "I really do love you, though. Didn't mean to ruin the moment, just wanted to share."

"Shhhhh." August kisses James once more, leaving one large finger against his lips, then starts turning him around to lay on his front. James goes gladly. August moves down his body, squeezing carefully once he reaches James's ass and spreading him apart with his talented hands. "How do you feel about cum play?"

"Oh my *god.*" James groans, hands sliding beneath the pillow to hold onto the edge of his mattress as August's mouth finds his rim. He can't believe this is his incredible life.

AFTER

Eleven years later...

"Uncle Jaaaames." William's voice makes it through the front door before he does. Clearly he's forgotten that he's meant to knock, even if it's only next door and James left it open for him.

"That you, Junior?" James turns around in his work chair and immediately gets up. The kid's responsible, but he's only eleven, and he wasn't supposed to be here for another fifteen minutes. Hopefully he didn't leave the house without telling his parents. Wouldn't be the first time.

"No, I'm a murderer." Will must have followed the sound of James's voice down the hall because he makes it to the doorway to the office at the same time as his uncle, running straight into him and throwing his arms around James in a hug.

"You been watching that true crime show without your parents again?" James ruffles his hair, smiling fondly at the way his nose scrunches exactly like Blair when they're annoyed. Some things transcend the limitations of genetics. "You know what your Opie said about that."

"Yes, but Uncle Karim said it's *important that I have freedom to explore intellectual pursuits that aren't dictated by my parents* and it doesn't show anything too scary." Will sounds far too much like a grown up with that answer, and James decides that maybe it's best to reroute the conversation before it goes down a parenting rabbit hole he's not prepared for.

"Your Uncle August won't be home for a few minutes. You're early." James walks out of the office and through the hall, William following close behind. But then he realises that Junior showed up empty

129

handed. "Hang on a second, where's all your supplies for your project?"

"Opie and Dad are bringing Clara in a few minutes with all the stuff." William shrugs and takes one of the stools at the kitchen counter, James already opening the fridge to get out his favourite: chocolate milk. It's a treat he's only allowed sparingly, but James spoils the kid and he's not shy about it. "I didn't feel like waiting while they spent ten minutes getting ready to walk across a garden."

"It's a lot of stuff to carry, especially if you left your school work behind." James has to hide a smile because William certainly got his dad's wit. For such a young kid, he manages to keep them all on their toes. His teenage years should be interesting.

"Oh, I'm supposed to tell you that Uncle Karim and Uncle Arthur will be here in an hour with the twins." William kicks at the counter with his trainers as he waits for James to pour his Sunday afternoon treat into a tea cup. It started as a joke, when Junior would come over as a toddler for "tea time" with his uncles while his parents got a well deserved break. And they couldn't very well give him actual tea, but the tradition stuck and now any beverage he consumes at James's house must be in a teacup. Not a mug. Not a glass. A porcelain tea cup with a saucer.

"Let me guess, the project is due tomorrow and you just told your parents yesterday, so now we all need to help you get it done on time?" James gently slides the well loved cup across the counter, reminiscent of his bartending days in his younger years.

"It's technically due on Friday, but if I turn it in early I get extra credit." Junior's feet stop kicking as he takes a sip, careful and restrained despite his age and energy. "Need top marks, you know."

"You're eleven." James points out with a laugh, turning around to grab a drink for himself from the fridge.

"If I want to be a teacher like Uncle Karim, I have to do my best. Uncle Arthur said that only the smartest kids with the best marks get to be teachers." William sets aside his chocolate milk and hops off the stool, walking towards the living room with James close behind. He picks up both of their drinks to follow William's path through the house. The kid's a whirlwind, but James is more than used to Hurricane William by now.

A few years ago, when James and August started to actually make a decent amount of money, it was around the same time that Blair and Henri decided it was time to expand their family with another kid. After several months of long talks over way too much coffee and a healthy amount of vodka, the four of them purchased a split house with a proper garden together, something their younger selves could only dream of.

With the new living arrangement, the uncles could help with the kids, Henri and Blair could lower their housing costs while gaining room, and they'd retain their privacy while staying in London where they want to be. Karim and Arthur are still close by, a smaller, but equally loved home for them and their twins. James and August decided early on that they didn't want kids of their own, but they both adore being uncles, so this arrangement is genuinely perfect for everyone.

"You want to watch something until Uncle August gets back and your parents walk over?" James asks, already reaching for the remote to hand over. He's found that letting William choose what to watch, within reason, gives him some insight into the kid's mind without having to pry. Maybe Karim was onto something.

William chooses a nature documentary, an older one with David Attenborough narrating the scenery with his distinctive voice. The current scene is all about hummingbirds, and while James isn't particularly interested, he smiles as Junior sips his chocolate milk from his tea cup and follows the bright colours in awe.

It's moments like these when James can't believe how quickly Junior's grown. It seems like just yesterday his parents were leaving him for his first overnight visit with James so that they could enjoy a date night. There've been dozens, maybe even hundreds of similar nights since then, and not just for Junior, but for Clara and for the twins, too. It's one of James's favourite things about being an uncle.

August gets home from his meeting a few minutes later, joining them in the living room with a hello kiss for James and a shoulder squeeze for Junior. James catches him up on the change in plans, including the expected list of guests and updated project timeline, all while massaging August's shoulders as he sits on the floor in front of him. August asks why they didn't just meet next door where all the supplies already live, but James doesn't have an answer and even if he did, he actually likes having the bright chaos that comes with their friends and their kids all showing up at once.

"Junior, come and help your Dad please." Blair's voice is next through the front door, holding it open so Clara can toddle her way inside. She's got a sippy cup in one hand and a toy firetruck in the other, immediately making her way over to August and asking to be picked up.

Clara's had a special connection to August since the first moment they met, in the same way James has a special bond with Junior. Sometimes kids pick a favourite; even though they love all their extended family, there's usually one person they sort of latch onto.

William rushes past Blair in the doorway and takes his school bag from Henri. There's craft supplies sticking out of it at odd angles, overflowing with way more than James thought would be needed for a simple year 6 school project. While setting his bag near the coffee table, Junior looks up at Henri to ask, "Did Opie remember the glitter?"

"I've got four different kinds, but you'll have to dig around in your bag. It's at the bottom." Blair answers, setting down everything else they've brought along for the kids. James and August's place is fully equipped, one of their guest rooms reserved for the four kids in case they ever spend the night. But their half of the house doesn't have

Junior's favourite hoodie or Clara's emotional support throw pillow (shaped like a heart with arms), amongst several other things that the kids could need at a moment's notice.

"Karim says they're leaving soon." Blair adds to James who's just greeted them with a hug.

"Should I be planning to feed everyone? Seems like this may take a few hours..." James glances back at where William's craft supplies have somehow exploded across the living room, poster board and paint and glue and all four types of glitter surrounding him while August and Henri pass Clara back and forth as she giggles.

"We'll figure it out, but probably." Blair reaches forward and moves Junior's leftover chocolate milk out of the way only a moment before it would've crashed to the floor, sighing and turning back to James with a smile. "Were you able to print out a few pictures? Junior insisted on at least five of everyone so he could have choices, but it's alright if you don't have that many."

"August took care of that bit, but he's got plenty. Says we'll just put the others somewhere around the house." James already made sure they had everything Junior asked for, but school projects tend to be one of those things where halfway through the kid remembers they suddenly need some random thing and someone has to panic run to the shops, so who knows.

"Opie, can you help me paint?" William seems to have selected which poster board he wants to use (the largest of the bunch), and now he's holding up a well loved paintbrush that used to belong to Arthur, staring at Blair with those puppy dog eyes. "It needs to be midnight blue and you're best at the colours."

"Maybe Uncle James could give us a hand?" Blair nudges James with their elbow, waiting for Junior to nod his head in agreement and search for a third paint brush. Arthur and Karim always have enough art supplies to hand down to the kids as they replace their own, and James is pretty sure the one he's been given used to be one of

133

Karim's watercolour brushes. They both have stressful jobs and their art helps them decompress, even if they don't get to do it as much since the twins entered their lives.

"You want to tell us more about your project?" James asks, carefully supporting his bad knee as he takes a seat on the floor near the soon to be painted poster. Part of being in his mid thirties is having all sorts of old injuries show back up again.

"Have to wait until my other uncles are here to explain." Junior is fully concentrating on choosing between two different shades of blue. James is of very little help because they look nearly identical, but Blair mumbles encouraging things that seem to help William decide which one to use. Pausing while deep in thought, Junior mutters to himself, "Paint needs time to dry."

"It's like a family tree, but Junior's changed it." Henri answers, looking through one of the bags he brought along for more of Clara's toys. If she isn't well occupied several feet away, she'll decide she needs to help her big brother and that will *not* end well. William takes his school work incredibly seriously, and as much as he loves Clara and is a wonderful older brother, he's still only eleven and learning how to manage emotions.

"It's a constellation." William adds to his dad's explanation, but leaves it at that. James decides it can wait, like Junior asked, because he seems very intent on getting the base layer of paint done ASAP and keeps getting those frustrated frowny looks whenever he's interrupted.

While they wait for the others to arrive, William manages to paint the entire surface with a deep, inky blue, then very thoroughly covers it with a base layer of miniscule silver glitter. He applies it all so carefully that only a few pieces end up on the floor, which is a small miracle on its own. "Dad, I need help."

"Give me a moment." Henri passes off Clara playmate duties fully to August (who was already serving as fire chief to Clara's three toy dinosaurs and exactly one Barbie in a ballgown) and scoots along the floor to be closer to the school work. Meanwhile, James and Blair are busy planning dinner so none of the kids get hangry without warning. Or the adults, if they're honest.

"You have the biggest family in the constellation." Junior holds up a blank piece of printer paper and a pencil in Henri's direction, shuffling a few feet away from the still damp poster board and waiting for his dad to follow. "Can you help me do a practice one on here?"

"Why don't we start with a list and then we can decide who needs to go where, hm?" Henri suggests, Junior nodding in response and starting to give his dad directions and listing everyone he can remember that needs to be included. Soon enough, Clara starts to droop as August continues his silly voices, so he passes her off to Blair to get her settled for a nap in the kids' room down the hall.

Karim and Arthur show up with the twins just after Clara falls asleep, entering much more calmly than the Tompson-Storey household. Karim opens the door and waits for Yamar and Tahira to walk in carrying their tiny backpacks with Arthur just behind.

The twins have always been a bit more reserved than their cousins, even as babies, very little fussing and well occupied playing together a majority of the time. And today's no different, going around the room for a hug from each person before settling in the spot Clara vacated and taking their own things out of their bags. Tahira's working on an animal colouring book and Yamar brought age appropriate legos to build. The three kids start up their own conversation, completely ignoring the adults, so the parents and uncles settle across the sofas a few feet away and just let the kids be.

"Quiet morning at yours?" James slings an arm around August, directing his question to Karim and Arthur who actually look a bit put out today.

"Hardly. Ta had a full blown meltdown about her pancakes." Arthur runs a hand down his face and leans into Karim for support. "Which then set Yamar off about wanting to watch telly instead of eating breakfast at the table. Wasn't even sure we were going to make it out the door but eventually we got them sorted."

"Arthur managed the pancakes and I distracted from the telly, but some mornings I wonder if you two aren't the smartest of the lot." Karim sets his head on Arthur's shoulder and a hand on his knee. "You get to be the cool uncles and hand them off when they start crying."

"I'm glad you're finally appreciating my genius." James grins, letting his fingertips stroke along August's bicep through his henley. "But without you we wouldn't have four incredible kids staining our carpets and finger painting on our walls, so where would we find our joy?"

"You didn't have to frame that, you know." Blair is cuddled up against Henri, the two of them in the middle of the others. It's nice that the kids are old enough at eleven, six, and three that they can give their parents a few spare minutes to breathe once in a while. Like now.

"Course we did." August nuzzles further into James out of habit, his curls against James's chest as he reclines while he can. They all know the calm won't last. "Clara's a little artist already. It's a masterpiece."

The three older kids keep at their activities and the others share a round of tea until Clara shuffles her way into the living room with her heart pillow, wiping sleep from her eyes and asking for her Uncle Karim to play school with her. He does, of course, giving her pretend school work to keep her occupied so Junior can keep making progress on his actual project. There's a snack break not long after before the kids run around in the garden with their Uncle James while the others clean up, then back in the house to finish William's project as a collective.

"Alright, Junior. What's next?" James helps William spread the mostly dry glittery poster out on the coffee table, hoping to get this thing finished at some point before school starts in the morning.

"I need pictures and I have to put names on these stars and I go in the middle and everyone goes around me." William holds up a small bag of silver star stickers and a picture of himself from a few weeks ago at the park. "Also it's a presentation so I'm supposed to know the stories about the pictures and explain how we're related. I couldn't do a tree because my family isn't like a tree, so Opie helped me decide what to do instead and I like glitter."

"Who's first?" Arthur asks with Tahira on his hip. He's busy zooming her around the room playing superheroes. Yamar makes an adorably ferocious Godzilla, stomping around after them with claw hands waving through the air. The kid is *obsessed* with heroes ever since he found out that his dads have a comic book collection. How he missed all the other nerd stuff at their house until this point is a mystery, but if he wants to play superheroes until he runs himself to exhaustion, they won't complain.

"How about we get us and my family on there first, and then Aunt Jen and Nana Pam?" Henri reaches for Junior's bag to find the envelope with the pictures of the Tompson-Storey family members all ready to go.

"And Papa Dan and Papa Ronnie." Junior adds, incredibly seriously, as if Henri leaving off their names from his casual list was like excluding them from a birthday party invite.

"Got their pictures right here." Henri assures him, giving Will a very specific, fond look because while he may be eleven and a personality and a half, he's got all the heart of his parents and then some.

The pictures of William, his family, The Tompson-Storey wedding, the day each of them came home with their parents, the entire Tompson family at Christmas, Blair's family from last summer, and special pictures of all their loved ones who've already died (some before Junior got to meet them) all get placed very carefully by Junior's growing hands. He dabs just a bit of glue on the back corners with Karim's help and smooths them in place before adding a star with each person's name beside their picture, August's steady handwriting filling in the names as they go.

After Junior's immediate family is taken care of, he decides it's Arthur and Karim's turn. They give him a picture from their wedding, one from their uni days when they'd just started dating, and one with the twins from their holiday to Barcelona last year. William lines up all three while listening to Arthur talk about how the twins came into their life, how Karim's older sister was their surrogate, Yamar adding his own commentary about the Barcelona trip for Junior to include and then yammering about his Auntie Neha until he gets distracted by something outside.

Karim tells Junior how they met at uni and where they took that earliest picture: in Arthur's uni flat that he shared with James. Tahira points at the wedding picture and tells William they have the same one at home above their fireplace, before mentioning that Leia (the family cat) knocked it over this morning. This is apparently news to her dads, but somehow unsurprising.

The twins adopted her as a kitten from the shelter as a sixth birthday present, agreeing on her name after watching *Star Wars* with their parents. Apparently the cat's white fur reminded Tahira of Leia's outfit, and Yamar likes to make lightsaber noises and run around, so it seemed fitting. It's been months of everything knocked over and curtains climbed and the most wonderful moments of the twins learning to live with and love their first pet.

"Mind if we stick around for dinner?" Arthur asks as Junior works on the finishing touches of their portion of the constellation, satisfied with their answers and the pictures provided.

"Already planned for it." James takes his phone out of his pocket and hands it over, the menu for one of their go-to takeout restaurants open with the others' orders already added. "We should probably order before we're done. It'll be mayhem once they're not distracted anymore."

Arthur nods, scrolling and choosing what he knows the kids will actually eat before asking Karim what he wants and taking care of that as well. He makes sure his family goes first, in everything. It's how Arthur's always been.

"Uncle James!" William must be done with the Das-Anderson pictures because he's staring at James expectantly, waiting for him to get the hint and join him back on the floor, preferably with what he needs next.

"Your Uncle August has the pictures." James grins at Junior's impatience. He's so much like his dad sometimes it's almost funny. That same little flick of his hair and set of his mouth.

"Uncle August!" William turns to him instead, glue in one hand like he'll start to panic if he can't affix another image to his constellation immediately.

"Left them in the study, just to be safe." August ruffles Junior's hair, leans down to kiss James at the temple, and leaves the room to retrieve the envelope of pictures he'd had printed for the occasion, then stored in chronological order. James adored the process of selecting which pictures to include in the project. They reminisced over their life together as they went through their digital albums, reliving their memories and deciding what to share.

As James watches August walk back into the room, he catches his eye and falls in love all over again in an instant. Continuously, repeatedly, infinitely bound to this person in ways he still struggles to articulate. August is both anchor and wave, someone James can't believe he's had over a decade to love and even more still to come. He never thought he'd be the type to cry through his wedding ceremony, and yet...

"Come sit with us for a minute, Junior." James pats the bit of floor between himself and where August's just sat down, waiting for William to huddle up into their space. "We couldn't decide so we'll tell you the stories and you can pick."

"I'm very good at decisions. Opie says it's one of my best qualities." Junior states with the confidence of someone who knows they're loved to the depth of their soul, even if they say words like *qualities* without knowing what it really means out of context.

"You have very strong opinions, yes." Blair is sitting with Tahira a few feet away, the look they share first with Henri and then with James incredibly amused. "You get that from your father."

Henri rolls his eyes but James knows he's secretly pleased.

"What's this one?" Junior's already back to the task at hand, his focus either crystal clear or scattered like birdseed. Right now it's the former.

"First night at our old flat, right after August moved in." James grins at the memory, the glow of the telly illuminating their faces as they turned sideways on the sofa to grin at James's phone for the selfie. He's pretty sure it was sent to Henri, but it could've been any of them. "Right after we met."

William takes the picture in his hand and squints for a minute, then sets it to the side in a way that very much communicates: no, thank you. "You don't look right…not like I know you."

"Sheesh. Observant kid." August teases, looking up at William's parents with a short laugh. "Your Uncle James wasn't my boyfriend yet in that picture. We were just friends, actually not even friends yet. Mostly strangers who decided to live together in the city."

Junior nods as if understanding why that picture won't work, already reaching for the next one in August's overlarge hand. When William was still a baby, August could cradle his entire head in just his palm, soothing and rocking him to sleep when he and James would babysit.

"That was one of your Uncle August's first gigs before, well, everything." James catches August's eye and silently asks for him to elaborate. This part of the story is his to tell.

"I didn't used to play cool shows like you see now. This one was at a cafe, but not the one I used to work at. Just an open mic night where I showed up and put my name on the list to get on stage." August remembers it so clearly. James was the only one who supported him that day, the only person in the audience there for *him*, and James's loud, almost obnoxiously loud, cheering as he left the tiny makeshift stage gave him enough confidence to do it again. And again and again and again until he started to make a name for himself about a decade ago. "Your Uncle James took that picture and printed it out for me with a little note on the back, asking me to sign it because he knew my signature would be worth something someday."

Flipping the picture over, William looks for the mentioned note but finds it blank. His forehead scrunches again, like he's trying to figure out where it went.

"That's just a copy, but the story is the same." James clarifies, the original print tucked safely in August's nightstand between the pages of his favourite book. James's first published collection of poetry had been dedicated to him:

For August, The muse I didn't realise I was missing because you were standing right in front of me, waiting to be seen. Your love has inspired every word.

August had that dedication engraved in James's handwriting on a silver pendant that he wears during every performance. If William looks closely at the last picture in the envelope, he'll see that same necklace managing to catch the light, but for now it's August in comfortable jeans and a plain black shirt, young and nervous in the back corner of a dingy cafe.

141

"...maybe." William sets it on top of the other already denied photo, but he does so carefully. Clearly he recognises it's an important story even if he doesn't want to use it for his project. "You're not in it, though, Uncle James."

"Feels like I am." James glances at August, thinking about how that picture was one of the many, many things that he saw with an entirely new perspective once he and August got together. Even then, so early on, the way he felt for August was well past platonic.

"Here. This is from the day after our first date. Your Uncle Arthur took this one." August hands over a third picture for Junior to examine, thinking they might be on the right track now for Junior's project. The kid really does know exactly what he's looking for.

"That's better!" Junior's eyes finally stop squinting as he looks at the two of them from long ago: James's arm around August's shoulders while they sit on what used to be Karim and Arthur's living room sofa. It lives in their bedroom now, occupied by the twins on nights they get scared by a storm or just won't sleep in their own room.

"In our old flat, before we had the twins. Your Uncle James dragged his new boyfriend out of bed so he could come gossip with me about the date, which might be the gayest thing he's ever done." Karim remembers aloud with a smirk.

He and Arthur moved into their house once the process of the surrogacy was certain. It was the gift of a lifetime, Karim's older sister agreeing with very little hesitation because she didn't plan to have kids of her own, but was happy to go through all of that both for her future niblings, and for the brother she loves more than anything. A few months after buying their new house (tiny but perfect), the twins were on their way home, Neha staying with Karim and Arthur for the first few months as they all adjusted to a new world.

"Your uncles couldn't take their eyes off each other that day. They were embarrassing." Karim gives James a tilted grin as he thinks back on time of their lives with fondness.

"We were adorable." James counters, frowning at Karim but then cracking a smile almost immediately. He knows Karim loves every single inch of him, even when he's prickly.

"What's wrong with Uncle August's neck?" Junior tilts his head as he tries to figure it out and James flushes in realisation while Henri cackles and does absolutely nothing to help. Maybe they should've checked the pictures more thoroughly.

"Probably just a bug bite." August clears his throat and distracts William with another picture. "Here. This was the day I signed with my agent. James took us all out to celebrate. Pretty sure your Auntie Dee babysat you that night. It was just after she moved to London."

"Too many people." Junior shakes his head no straight away, but instead of putting it off into the reject pile with the others, he turns to the side and holds it up to his dad. "Can we put this one on the fridge, please? I like it."

"Course we can. I'm sure there's still room somewhere." Henri looks over at his spouse who just smiles and shakes their head. The fridge has been Junior's newest canvas, adding everything from his dad's random notes about groceries to his little sister's scribbles from nursery. The surface is getting a bit full, but it's harmless and endearing how he wants to show his family how much he loves them in this very specific, bizarre way.

"You're with us in this one." James takes the next picture from August and holds it in front of William where he's still sitting between them. In the photo, he and August are in matching suits, crouching down to be at Junior's level for a selfie. It ended up being the best picture they got with William the entire day, more natural and candid than anything the hired photographer got of the three of them. "You remember our wedding? You were only about five."

143

"This is definitely going on the constellation." William holds it for only a moment before setting it between his crossed legs like it was the easiest decision he's ever made. "Was I your flower girl?"

James smiles wide but shakes his head no. Back when they were planning the wedding, Junior asked to be their flower girl, but apparently he doesn't remember. James and August had decided against anything traditional and didn't even have wedding parties since they only invited their closest mates and a handful of family members, the total guest list a baker's dozen of attendees.

They made sure that Junior had a flower crown as requested, even if his services weren't required for the ceremony. "No, but you helped your Uncle Arthur hold the rings for us until we needed them."

"Oh! I remember!" William reaches out to August's wedding ring right beside him and only stops a few inches away as if remembering he's supposed to ask before grabbing people like that. "Think it was the first wedding I went to."

"It was." August slides his ring off his finger and lets Junior hold onto it for a minute. If he could handle the responsibility as a five year old, he can handle it temporarily now. "This is one of my favourite pictures. Happiest day of my life."

"I had three slices of cake!" William suddenly remembers, fidgeting with August's ring as he keeps talking. "And Opie said I was going to fly myself to the moon if I had any more sugar and then I tried to climb really tall but Dad caught me before I fell...still think I could've done a pretty good jump if I tried again."

"You left your wings at home that day." Henri sticks his tongue out at William, waiting for him to do it back. He's at that age where he tries to act all cool around his school friends, but here, in one of his homes, he's still silly and relaxed and childish. So he returns his dad's expression, scrunching up his face in exactly the same way until they're both laughing. With one last giggle, he hands back

August's ring very carefully, like he's worried it might break if he drops it.

"Here. Two more." August takes out a picture of himself and James laughing together on their first anniversary, the Paper Anniversary, when he'd gotten James a joke gift and James managed to write an entire memoir about their lives together in secret, had it printed and lovingly signed, and used a picture of them saying their vows as the cover image. Their first anniversary has been a foundational memory ever since.

"Books? Your books?" William turns to James, then glances over towards the study where there's a bookshelf containing about a dozen copies of each of James's published books. Four so far, with a fifth in the works.

"Yes and no." James stands up from the floor and walks into the study to retrieve both of the books shown in the picture. They have a place of honour on the shelf between their desks: James's neat with just his laptop and a glass for water, August's a mess of things with a laptop somewhere in the pile. Somehow, even though James writes words and August sings them, they've been able to share a home office since the day August moved into James's bedroom at their old flat and his bedroom became the spare. No more typing away at the kitchen table or practising sets on the sofa. Unless they wanted to, of course.

"Careful with these. They're the only copies." James hands William his gift to August first. He'd worked on it for almost six months before sending it off to be printed, asking Karim to act as editor for this one, very special work that he would *never* share with the world. He trusted Karim with it more than anyone, and not just because of his job. "Each wedding anniversary has a different theme, and the first wedding anniversary is the paper anniversary, so I wrote a book just for your Uncle August. I told our whole story from the first time we met until our honeymoon in Japan. That's what he's holding in the picture."

"Best if you just skim the contents." Karim adds helpfully from where he's marking Clara's pretend schoolwork. She earns top marks, of course.

With that, James remembers some of the more explicit chapters and carefully shifts the book so Junior's looking at the back cover where there's another picture of them, but this time from their honeymoon with the blossoming cherry trees like a sort of halo above their beaming faces. That trip lives like a talisman in James's soul, always there when he needs to remember that life can be full of love and joy and adventure.

"Does everyone give books to their husbands?" William asks so earnestly that none of the adults in the room can find it in themselves to laugh. It's sort of incredible to know a child like this. Like any of their kids.

"No, not everyone. And some people have wives." James grips Junior's shoulder for a moment. He loves William as if he's one of his own. In a way, he is, because his parents have been family since before he was born.

"Like Ms. Baker!" Junior nods, as if he should've remembered. Ms. Baker is the teacher who set this assignment, but James hadn't realised she has a wife. "She got married to Ms. Bailey over the summer. So they'll write books like this, too?"

"They might, but not everyone celebrates in the same way." James gently takes back the book he wrote for August, ready to swap it for the other in just a minute. "And sometimes boys marry girls, too. And nonbinary people can marry whoever they want. Or not get married. Not everyone wants to get married."

"Opie married my dad but they said they didn't have a choice." Junior looks to Blair to confirm. They laugh for a moment, picking up Clara to go play outside again because she's getting antsy.

"I didn't put it quite like that, but I did say that meeting your dad was fate. He's my soulmate. I was always going to marry your dad." Blair rifles through the bag of things they brought with them until they find Clara's jumper. The temperature's fallen now that the day's almost over. "No matter what, I would've chosen him. I'd still choose him if we met today for the first time."

Henri can't respond to that the way he'd like right now, but he moulds himself to the side of Blair not currently occupied by their toddler to whisper something private and kiss the side of their mouth, one hand in their short curls while the other joins the hand holding Clara on their hip. Sometimes James wonders how they're still like this, almost two decades into a relationship. He doesn't believe in soul mates as a concept, but he also thinks Blair might be on to something.

"Dog's outside?" Clara asks, and no one is surprised because it's all she can talk about lately. One of their neighbour's dogs had gotten loose and found its way into their shared garden, and Clara didn't understand that it couldn't stay. It's enough to make her dads consider finally getting one after putting it off for years.

"Not today, ducky." Blair helps her into her jumper with Henri's assistance then turns back to the twins. "You two want to come outside with us?"

"Can we play superheroes again?" Yamar asks, already standing up to follow regardless of the answer. And once Tahira sees her brother get up, she doesn't want to be left out. Henri follows Blair like they're magnetically linked, and Karim and Arthur give the three left on the floor a look then follow everyone else.

"Here." August reaches across Junior to take the other book from James so he can leaf through it with him. Now that the younger kids are outside there's marginally less chaos in the room, but the sounds of laughter and playtime find their way inside through the back door. "Mine wasn't nearly as fancy or emotional as James's book. He had this job back in the day where he would write horoscopes for a magazine. You know what those are?"

"Magazines? Heard of them." William answers, and James genuinely can't tell if he's taking the piss. It's not as if he wrote his posts on a typewriter and stood at the newsstand to see it in print. Even back then it was all digital.

"Horoscopes." August stifles a laugh. He knew they were getting old, but being around the youth is always a stark reminder.

"Like stars and stuff, yeah? Constellations, but not like mine. It's got glitter." Junior straightens his posture proudly, pointing over at his almost completed project.

Once August and James's pictures and corresponding stars are added, it's all set to be handed over to the teacher in the morning. William told them earlier that when he has to take it back home from school he's going to hang it up in his bedroom because he doesn't have any family pictures in there yet, only the ones his parents have around the rest of the house.

"Similar to yours, in some ways. The ones people use for horoscopes sort of came from the Greeks a long time ago, and each constellation has stories and things that go with it. The horoscopes I wrote were all made up nonsense, but for some people astrology is very real." James shrugs. It's not his place to judge anyone else's belief system as long as no one is getting hurt. "Anyway, your dad is the reason I asked August on a date in the first place."

"James used to write the horoscopes for his friends, like your parents and your uncles and me. Here, look at the first page." August taps the top of the book to encourage Junior to open it.

Not nearly as elaborate as James's contribution, August had taken a nice leather-bound journal, printed out all of James's horoscopes for Leo, and added his own commentary where he saw fit. The glue's held almost everywhere, but a few of the horoscopes are starting to peel up at the edges. "I'm a Leo because my birthday is August 18th, and what your dad realised is that the way James would write horoscopes for Leo wasn't like a friend. More like a partner, or a boyfriend in James's case. Because he was in love with me, but he just didn't realise yet."

"Neither did you." James huffs automatically, but he starts flipping through the pages until he finds one of the early ones he remembers. "Also Henri wasn't the only one who realised, but he's the first one who said something to me. Your dad showed me a bunch of these tweets, like this one, and gave me a bit of a talk, and a month later August and I had our first date. You were still a baby so you wouldn't remember, but we were at your first Pride parade with you that same year and it was both of our first Pride after coming out, so your uncles and your parents made a big deal of it and had all three of us wear matching *Baby's First Pride* shirts."

"Opie has a picture near the stairs." Junior points vaguely in the direction of his own home, as if they can see the placement of the photo through the wall that divides the houses. They've seen it many times, of course, but it's been there so long it's almost faded into the background. James is surprised Junior remembers it. "So you used to write little love notes to Uncle August but pretended they were about the stars?"

James laughs, reaching his arm past Junior to thread it through the curls at the back of August's head and give him a soft smile. "I did, yeah. It started before we were dating but I kept doing it until I gave up the job. And your Uncle August printed them all out and hand wrote his own love notes in response for our anniversary."

"Why'd you stop writing them?" William keeps flipping through the book, not really reading anything, just taking it in. There's a *lot* of horoscopes.

"Didn't need the job anymore." James's hand in August's hair keeps caressing him absentmindedly while the three of them stare down at the book together. "Started writing songs for August to sing and my

149

first book got picked up by a publisher. Kept on at the bar for a bit, but even that didn't last much longer. Turns out August and I make a pretty great team, and not just as husbands."

"No kissing." William wrinkles his nose but he doesn't scoot away from them. He closes the book and hands it back to James, satisfied with what he's learned about their story from its pages.

"Still think kissing is gross, hm?" August teases, searching the floor at his side for the last picture they'd chosen.

Junior's teetering on the edge of becoming a teenager, and fast. Before they know it he'll be going on dates of his own and getting embarrassed about his crushes, if he has them. In a few years he'll be driving! And then it'll be off to uni or travelling the world or whatever he decides. Hard to believe that it's been over a decade since he became their first nibling.

"...not always." Junior flushes red and crosses his arms over his chest defensively. "Sometimes it seems alright."

James is the cool uncle, so he doesn't comment on that. Junior will share when he's ready. He always does.

"Last picture." August sets aside the now empty envelope and lets William examine the final option. "Backstage after I played at the Roundhouse in Camden. James waited backstage for me the entire time while you were up in VIP with your other uncles and the twins, wearing those big headphones. But your Opie took this picture of us when I rushed off stage at the end of the show and hugged James right away. It's pretty great, with the stage lights and the crowd behind us, but if you don't want to use it - "

"I'm using it." Junior cuts him off, his pointer finger tracing the lines of the curtains like he's remembering how they felt in his slightly smaller hands almost two years ago. After most of the crowd had left, the whole family (August's parents and sisters included) met backstage and August took all the kids out onto the stage to look around at the empty venue, Clara on his hip and the others all walking around at their own pace, exploring. He's played similar venues since, but that was his first truly big, headlining show.

"You have what you need?" James checks with William, because they're out of pictures, but if he absolutely had to find some others, they could somehow get them before the morning.

"Think so. This one and the wedding picture and the one with the books." Junior stands up from the floor for the first time in several minutes and kneels next to his almost complete project on the coffee table. Confident as always, he arranges the three pictures in the blank corner of his poster and leans back to look at the whole thing. "Like this."

"I think it's perfect." August glances over William's shoulder at the entire constellation. It's honestly really well done, and something Junior should be proud of.

"We love you, Junior. Everyone in your constellation loves you." James leans down to kiss the top of William's head. He doesn't have to lean quite as far as he's used to anymore. One day he'll probably be taller than James and then what's he to do?

"...love you too." William mumbles a few seconds too late because he's back to being very focused on his work. With Karim outside it's up to him to get the pictures glued in place just right. August still helps with the stars because Junior said the handwriting absolutely had to be consistent, but all of the sudden, what had been a huge undertaking is complete.

Literally the second he's finished, William rushes past them to go out into the garden with the others, immediately joining in on the fun. James and August follow after him, holding hands as they step outside to spend time with the family before dinner.

Sundays for August and James used to mean long nights working at the pub or early nights in before dawn shifts at the cafe, squeezing in time to see their friends and each other while trying to get by. But now Sundays are chasing kids around their garden, crowding ten people around a table meant for eight, and tea and a chat for the grownups after the kids fall asleep in the other room.

After everyone's left for the night and they've tidied the house, James pulls his husband into their study and takes down that book with all the horoscopes he'd written for August to revisit together, now that they're alone.

"Haven't looked at these in a while." James has August in his lap even though the loveseat in their home office has plenty of room for them to sit side by side. He generally prefers August as close as he can have him. They still centre each other with their physical presence, with their touch, their voice, their energy. Some things haven't changed over the years, even with how different their lives are here, in this house, stable in their chosen careers and happy with their favourite person. "Can't believe this is where it all started for us."

"I can." August leans back against his husband, the book open in his hands while he rereads some of his favourite posts. He's got them memorised by now, but there's something about the physicality of the book that gives them more weight. "You loved me before you even realised, and I'm lucky enough to have proof."

"Luck's got nothing to do with it. I wrote every single one of these very intentionally. I knew who I was writing them for and how incredible he was…still is" James kisses the side of August's neck and sighs. "I think I did know I loved you, even before I realised. Think we both did."

"True." August slides the book closed and off his lap, then turns himself around in James's arms. Nostalgia never seems to pull them in even if they enjoy their reminiscing. As lovely as their memories are, their current life is so brilliant and everything they yearned for that the past is less like a temptation than a foundation: less visible

152

but always there. "Ravish me on the sofa before you take me to bed?"

"Those kids have me worn out." James laughs, but he's already standing up and taking August by the hand to walk him back into the living room and do exactly that. "But I think I could still find it in me."

"Could probably inspire you." August pulls James into him for a kiss, not wanting to wait until they're horizontal. He loves a long, indulgent snog, and James loves to spoil him. They're a match made in heaven or out among the stars, somewhere far off and beautiful if the way they love each other is any indication.

"You always do, Augie." James presses August by the shoulders until he's laying back against the sofa cushions. The way he looks up at James is like nothing else, like James is the centre of his universe and the most beautiful soul he'll ever know. It's a lot to live up to, but he does his best. "Don't have to be in the studio until the afternoon tomorrow?"

"Nope. Not til two." August smirks, already knowing where this is headed. "I'm all yours, babe."

"Been a while since we had time to play all morning." James presses a kiss to August's lips, then his jaw, down his neck, slipping his hands beneath August's shirt so he can get it out of their way. "You're still the perfect man for me. All these stories and pictures made me remember how far we've come. I love you more in every single way than I ever could've imagined at the beginning. Didn't have a clue what we were in for, but I knew I wanted to find out."

He keeps kissing and caressing August's body as he talks, fingertips gentle on August's skin to distract him from focusing on James's lips. He wants to drag this out as long as he can. August is already squirming impatiently but James intends to make him wait. They're in no rush tonight.

"Keep talking." August groans, shifting himself on the sofa so James can have easier access to play with him however he wants. James knows how August loves his voice and the commanding tone he takes when they're having sex, but it's nice to hear him ask. "Please."

It's quite a while before they finally make it to the bedroom, indulging in each other and the security that's been built during a decade of choosing one another and their relationship time and time again. It hasn't always been easy or simple or without obstacles, but it's always, *always* been worth it. This, them together, it's always been right. They have a genuine partnership, a lasting connection built on a solid foundation of trust, and it all started with a tiny flat, afternoon chats over pastries, and supporting the other from the very beginning.

When they're done fucking for the night and they're laying all twisted up in bed, James extricates himself long enough to open the curtains so they can stare up at the night sky together. The moon is bright and the clouds have retreated, at least momentarily, which is a rare thing in the city.

"Love you in all of those." August kisses James's bare chest above his heart and stares out the window with him, sharing his gaze. "Every universe."

And then he's asleep before James can find a response. He kisses August's temple and holds him close, imagining all those versions out themselves that might be out there somewhere. Maybe August's a pilot in one, James an artist in another, some variant of themselves that always finds their way together. It's a nice thought, but it's more than that. It's undeniable, somehow.

James doesn't believe in the multiverse or in horoscopes or really any system of faith. But he believes in August and he doesn't have to believe in their relationship because he knows it, more true than he knows anything, so deep in his soul that he's certain.

"Every single one." James finally answers, even though August's been snoring on his chest already for several minutes. August will still hear him, somehow. He'll know James's love even in his sleep. James stays up a while longer, trailing fingers through August's curls and pressing soft kisses to his face, dreaming while wide awake.

They've had eleven years already and there's decades more to look forward to. What will the rest of their lives bring?

Acknowledgements

This work was originally inspired by a tumblr post by an anonymous user via an ask box to batmanisagatewaydrug-deactivate. While the story I wrote varies almost entirely from that post, the idea of having James write horoscopes for August blossomed from seeing that post somewhere on Twitter. Imagining the two of them telling their origin story to Junior is what sold me on the concept.

My writing would not be possible without every reader who has supported my work from the very first word, and especially those who reached out with endless encouragement.
I would not be the writer or person I am today without the online communities who have shaped me, and for that, I will always be grateful.

I also owe quite a debt to the friends who have edited drafts, encouraged ideas, and talked me through the tough decisions related to being an independent author. You all know who you are. I love you.

As a quick aside, I want to be clear that I'm not intending for this story to mock those who follow astrology or related belief systems. James's approach is his own and meant to reflect a general attitude towards fate and predisposition consistent with his character.

BT

About the Author

Briar Townsend is a writer, a reader, and about a dozen other things. Mostly, they are a human who is doing their best. Briar is unapologetically queer and neurodivergent. They find value in writing the stories they always wished to read and representing identities that often go unacknowledged by the mainstream.

***

Contact: briar.townsend.official@gmail.com

Website: briartownsend.com

www.ingramcontent.com/pod-product-compliance
Lightning Source LLC
Chambersburg PA
CBHW050401110726
47899CB00008B/2606